Retta had gotten up and started for home. Halfway there she began running, stumbling over the sidewalk even though she knew every crack and buckle. She had come into the house, flushed, out of breath, to find her father with his guitar. . . . It seemed that all her life, at every vital moment, Shorty Anderson had been composing a song.

She had stood there, heart pounding so hard she couldn't hear the words he was singing. And she had suddenly felt as if she were seeing her father so clearly that her image of him might be damaged forever, the way one's eyes are damaged by looking directly at the sun.

BETSY BYARS is the author of many books for children. Among them are *The Summer of the Swans*, awarded the Newbery Medal in 1971, and *The House of Wings* and *The Cartoonist*, both available in Yearling editions.

THE NIGHT SWIMMERS

Betsy Byars

For Sloane and Cole

LAUREL-LEAF BOOKS bring together under a single imprint out-standing works of fiction and nonfiction particularly suitable for young adult readers, both in and out of the classroom. Charles F. Reasoner, Professor Emeritus of Children's Litera-ture and Reading, New York University, is consultant to this series.

Published by
Dell Publishing
a division of
Bantam Doubleday Dell Publishing Group, Inc.
666 Fifth Avenue
New York, New York 10103

ISBN: 0-440-96776-X

RL: 5.3

Reprinted by arrangement with Delacorte Press
Printed in the United States of America
August 1981

10
KRI

When the swimming pool lights were turned out and Colonel and Mrs. Roberts had gone to bed, the Anderson kids came out of the bushes in their underwear. They moved silently over the moss-smooth lawn, across the Moroccan tiled terrace.

At the edge of the pool they stopped. Retta, the girl, said, "See, I told you it was beautiful." She stared at the shimmering water as proudly as if she had made the pool instead of just discovered it one day.

"But what if somebody sees us?" Roy asked. He hiked up his underwear uneasily. The elastic was sprung, and he wasn't sure the safety pin was going to hold.

"No one's going to see us. It's too dark." She

shrugged as if it didn't matter anyway. "The shallow end's down here. Come on."

She led them to the end of the pool, and together the three of them started down the steps.

"It's cold," Roy said. He clutched his underwear tighter, pulling it toward his chest.

"You'll get used to it."

Abruptly Johnny pulled away. "I want to go down the ladder," he said. He started around the pool.

Retta frowned slightly. Lately Johnny had started doing things his own way. "All right," she called after him, belatedly giving permission, "but then you swim right over to the shallow end, you hear me? I don't want to have to come in and save you."

"You won't." As Johnny took hold of the smooth metal ladder, an adult feeling came over him. He entered the water slowly—it was cold—and then pushed off. He dog-paddled to Retta and Roy, turning his head from side to side in a motion he thought made his dog paddle look more powerful.

"Now you two play here in the shallow end while I do some swimming," Retta said when Johnny joined them.

"I don't see why *I* have to stay in the shallow end," Johnny said.

"Because only one can go in the deep water at a time. That's a rule, and you already had your turn."

Beside them Roy was pretending to swim. He

had one hand on the bottom of the pool and was lifting the other arm in an elaborate swimming stroke. Then he put that hand on the bottom and lifted the other. "Want to see me swim, Retta?"

"That's nice, Roy," she said. She moved toward the deep end and began to swim silently. She was aware that Johnny was watching her, hoping to find fault, so she moved with deliberate grace. She copied the movements she had seen the Aquamaids do on television. She turned on her back. Then she swirled and dived under the water. Her bare feet rose, toes pointed, and shone in the moonlight.

Johnny was both impressed and irritated. Since he could find no fault with Retta, he looked down at Roy and said meanly, "You aren't really swimming."

"I am too!" Roy paused in the middle of the stroke to look back at Johnny.

"Your hand is on the bottom."

"It is not," Roy said. "Here's my hand right here."

"The other one is on the bottom."

Roy made a quick switch. "It is not. See, here's the other one."

"You aren't fooling anybody."

Johnny turned back to watch Retta. She was under the diving board now. She reached up and grabbed the board with both hands. She glanced around to see if Johnny and Roy were watching.

When she was sure they were, she skinned the cat and dropped into the water without a sound.

She swam to the side and pulled herself out of the water without bothering to use the ladder. Then she got the inflated mattress that Mrs. Roberts always used. She carried it to her brothers at the shallow end of the pool. "Want a ride?"

Roy paused in the middle of a swimming stroke; one arm was raised as high as if he wanted to be called on. "Is it all right if we use that?" he asked, peering at Retta from under his arm.

"Sure, get on."

The boys crawled onto the mattress and stretched out self-consciously. Their arms were stiff at their sides.

"I'll push you around the pool." Retta began to move the float into deeper water. "Doesn't it make you feel elegant?"

Johnny nodded. He was shivering in his wet underwear, chilled with the excitement and the evening air. He tried to relax, to feel the elegance Retta mentioned. He tried to imagine that he was a movie star in his own swimming pool. It began to work. He relaxed. He pantomimed smoking with a long cigarette holder.

"Aren't you glad you came?" Retta asked, spitting water out of her mouth. She was now in the deep water, kicking silently, moving the mattress under the diving board.

Roy reached up and touched the diving board.

Retta smiled. She had a wonderful feeling of belonging tonight, as if it really were her pool.

"Want to go around again?"

Without waiting for an answer, she turned the corner. Retta considered herself a sort of social director for her brothers. She often told them, "We're going to do all the things rich people do." Then she usually added, "Only we have to do them at night, that's the only difference."

Both of the boys were relaxing now. In the brief time they had been at the pool, they had come to associate the smell of chlorine with elegance. They breathed deeply as their sister pushed them through the water. Johnny had his hands folded behind his head, a pose he associated with famous people. Roy was waiting, arm lifted, to grab the diving board again.

Suddenly a light went on in the upstairs of the Roberts's house. The Anderson kids froze. All three faces turned to the window. Retta stopped kicking and waited, froglike, in the shimmering water.

"Retta!" Roy wailed. He turned to her. In the moonlight his twisted face revealed his fear. He was the youngest and the most sensitive to being caught.

"It's all right," Retta assured him. She reached forward and put her hand on his trembling shoulder. "That's just the bathroom light."

"How do you know?"

"I *know*. If you'd shut up, you could probably hear the toilet flush."

"I'm getting off this thing," Johnny said. He felt exposed. If somebody looked out the window, he thought, the first thing they would see would be him. The water was safer. He rolled off the mattress with a splash.

"Be quiet or they *will* hear us," Retta warned.

"Don't topple me!" Roy cried. He struggled to get in the middle, but the mattress tipped. With his arms clutching Retta's neck, he plopped into the water.

His head went under, and he came up sputtering. "Don't let me drown!"

"Shut *up*!" Retta said.

The three of them were at the side of the pool now. Johnny was holding on to the mattress; Retta was holding Roy. Their faces were turned up to the square of light above them.

"I'm scared," Johnny said. He was shivering hard now. His teeth began to chatter.

"There's nothing to be afraid of."

"Let's go home."

"Not yet."

"I *hate* it when people run us off," Johnny said.

"Me *too*," Roy said. He always spoke in a loud, positive voice when he was agreeing with his brother. "And I want to go home too!"

"Look, the reason people run you off is to *make* you feel bad," Retta explained. "They figure they'll run you off and you'll feel so bad that you won't come back. Only that is not going to work with us. We are going to swim here every night this summer."

While she was saying this, the light in the upstairs of the Roberts's house went out.

"See, I told you," Retta said. "It was the bathroom."

"I'm cold. I want to go." Johnny was the thinnest of the three and felt the cold most.

"We'll make one more lap of the pool and then we'll go. Come on, we'll all hang on to the mattress. Kick, everybody."

"I want to go. I'm cooooold," Roy wailed.

"Not yet," Retta said firmly. It was her policy never to leave at once. Even if the colonel had appeared in person and had yelled at them in a military voice, she felt she would still insist they make this one extra lap.

They kicked their way around the pool without speaking. Johnny was kicking with all his strength in order to get the swim over with. The only sound was the chatter of his teeth.

When they were back in the shallow end of the pool, Retta straightened. "*Now* we'll go home," she said.

She pulled the mattress out of the pool and set it where she had found it. "Come on," she told her brothers.

Together they ran across the lawn and got their clothes from the bushes. They pulled on their jeans as they walked under the trees. Retta had

come to like the feel of dry clothes pulled over
chilled wet skin.

"Didn't that make you feel good?" she asked.

Roy nodded. He was hopping on one foot,
trying to get the other foot into his pants leg. His
wet underwear sagged, and he yanked it up. Retta
held on to his elbow to steady him.

Then they moved together across the lawn, past
the rose garden, past the orchid greenhouse, past
the lemon trees from Florida, over the wall made
from stone from Mexico.

As she walked, Retta wore a faint, proud smile,
as if she were being cheered by an invisible
crowd.

The Anderson kids entered their house noisily. They called to each other. They snapped lights on and off as they moved to their bedrooms. Roy paused in the living room and turned on the television, but as soon as Retta heard *The Tonight Show* she came back and turned it off.

"Why not?" Roy whined.

"Because it's late. Now get to bed." She pointed with one hand to his bedroom. Her other hand was on her hip. When she stood like that, like a real mother, Roy knew there was no point in arguing.

"I never get to do anything!" he yelled. He stomped out of the room.

There was no reason for them to be quiet because the house was empty. Shorty Anderson, their father, was a country-western singer who worked at night. Their mother had been dead for two years, and Retta was raising the three of them.

"Want me to get you something to eat?" Retta asked. The success of the evening had made her feel more maternal than usual.

In the hall the sound of Roy's stamping feet stopped. "Peanut butter sandwich," he said quickly.

"Okay."

"*With* bananas."

"You want anything, Johnny?"

Johnny mumbled, "No," sleepily. He was already in his pajamas. He got in bed, rolled over, face to the wall, and fell asleep.

Beside him Roy was getting ready for his sandwich. He smoothed the sheet over his body as carefully as if it were a tablecloth. He wiped his hands, front and back, on his T-shirt. He loved to eat. The thought of the unexpected sandwich—Retta usually did not allow them to have bedtime snacks—made his face glow with pleasure.

"Kool-Aid too, please, Retta," he called out in a polite voice.

In the kitchen, in the bright light over the sink, Retta was humming under her breath. She was slicing the banana, placing the slices in neat rows on the peanut butter. In the window she could see her reflection, her long wet hair swinging about her face. She smiled at herself.

Retta was happier tonight than she had been in months. She had been taking care of her brothers all her life, but this summer, since they had moved to this neighborhood, it had become a lonely task. Tonight, however, they had had fun. She and her brothers were like friends now, she decided, doing things together. The summer vacation stretched ahead as one companionable, fun-filled day after another.

Retta finished making the sandwich, set it on top of a glass of milk, and carried it into her brothers' bedroom. "No Kool-Aid," she said firmly as she handed the sandwich and milk to Roy.

"Thank you." Roy was polite when it came to food. He said "please" and "thank you" without even knowing he was saying the words. In kindergarten he never had to be reminded by Miss Elizabeth, "Now, what do you say to Mrs. Hartley for the cupcakes?" because he gasped out, "Thank you," at the first glimpse of a white bakery box.

He turned his sandwich carefully, like a dog circling a bone. When he made his decision and took his first bite, an expression of contentment came over his face.

As usual, he began to eat the crust of the bread first. He nibbled around the sandwich, trying to be dainty. He believed that you got more if you ate daintily.

Retta leaned against the chest of drawers, watching him work his way around his sandwich. Just when he finished the last of the crust and was ready to sink his teeth into the peanut butter and banana, she said, "But, tomorrow, Roy, I'm putting you on a diet."

He was so startled that he almost dropped his sandwich. He looked at her. In the soft bread remained the horseshoe print of his teeth. "What?"

"I'm putting you on a diet tomorrow."

"Why?" It was a cry of pain. "I'm not fat."

"You have to wear Chubbies now. Before long you'll be in Huskies."

"I won't!"

"We'll talk about it tomorrow."

"I won't be in Huskies. I promise!"

"We'll talk about it in the morning," Retta said in the mature voice she had gotten from TV mothers.

"I promise I promise I promise—" He went up on his knees in a beggar's position. "I promise I promise I—"

"Will you shut up and lie still?" Johnny rose up on one elbow and gave Roy a look of disgust and anger. "I'm trying to sleep!"

"Well, I'm not going on a diet no matter what!" To emphasize his point he began to take huge bites of his sandwich, gnawing at the bread like an animal, poking stray bananas into his mouth with his finger. When his mouth was completely filled, a solid mass of banana, peanut butter, and bread, he folded his arms over his chest. He stared defiantly at Retta. He smacked. He chewed. He kept on working his jaws long after the sandwich had been eaten.

Then he sat, arms folded, staring at Retta. "Drink your milk," she said.

He drank it without pausing, eyes always on Retta.

"Now, good night," she said.

"Good night, *Loretta*," he called after her, wanting to hurt her and knowing how much she hated to be called by her full name. She alone resented that she had been named for a country singer. *Loretta Lynn!*"

She turned. "Good night, Roy *Acuff!*"

"*Loretta Lynn!*"

"Roy Acuff!"

"*Shut up!*" Johnny yelled. He sat up in bed and glowered at them both.

Roy lay down. "Johnny Cash," he said, just mouthing the words, silently taunting his brother.

He smoothed the covers over his stomach. It was nights like these, he thought, when he missed his mother most. Suddenly Roy imagined her coming into his room in one of her country-western outfits, the white satin one with the sequined guitars on the skirt.

In the daytime he could never remember what his mother looked like and stared at her photo-

graphs in vain. But on lonely nights he could remember every detail. Tonight she surprised him
by bringing with her a tray full of tiny cakes with
lighted candles on top. She was still coming to his
bed, smiling, when he fell asleep.

In the living room Retta was sitting on the
sofa. She picked up the evening paper. Usually
she went through the paper at night to check for
possible outings. She circled them in Magic Mark-
er, things like free Cokes at McDonald's, a wed-
ding reception at the Catholic church.

Tonight, however, she had no interest in such
minor events. Now she had the pool. And it was
only five blocks away—that was the best part—just
on the other side of the park.

Tomorrow, she thought, I'll get some inner
tubes at the filling station. Suddenly she sat up
straighter. And bathing suits! I'll get us bathing
suits!

The picture of them crossing the colonel's lawn
in bright new bathing suits was so clear, so beautiful, that she was determined to make it real.

She got up and went into the kitchen. Her father kept household money in the breadbox. She
opened the lid and counted. Seven dollars and
thirty-nine cents. She would need at least—she
paused, estimating—at least seventeen dollars.

She left the kitchen. As she passed her brothers'
room, she glanced in. The boys were both asleep:
Johnny, a long, thin line under the sheet; Roy, a
round ball.

"We," she told them quietly, "are going to have inner tubes *and* bathing suits." And she went into her room feeling as satisfied as if they already had them.

It was ten o'clock in the morning, and it was raining, a hard, solid rain, the kind that could go on
for days unless the wind shifted and the southwest
weather moved in.

Retta sat on the top step of the porch, eating a
piece of toast. She finished, licked her fingers, got
up, and went slowly into the house. She eased the
screen door shut behind her. Her father was asleep
in the front bedroom, and he did not like to
be awakened by slamming doors, loud television,
or shouting children.

She stood for a moment in the doorway. The living room was a mess. The furniture was faded and
worn. Newspapers and letters, some crumbled
into fist-sized balls, lay on the rugless floor. The

corner with the plastic leather armchair, her father's corner, was littered with plates piled with cigarette butts, half-filled coffee cups, and empty beer cans.

Retta was beginning to realize what a mess the house was, but she didn't know what to do about it. "We need a vacuum cleaner," she decided suddenly and felt better. She sat on the floor, cross-legged, and began to leaf through the newspaper.

"What are we going to do today?" Roy asked. He was standing in the doorway of the kitchen. He was happy because there had been no further mention of diets. Retta had even fixed his favorite, peanut butter toast, for breakfast. He pulled his jeans up higher on his hips and walked into the room.

"I'm looking for possibilities now," she said. She paused to work out her horoscope.

"We can't go swimming tonight because it's raining."

"I know that."

"So what are we going to do? I want to *do* something." He forgot his good fortune about the diet and broke into a whine.

"What you're going to do, if you don't shut up, is wake Dad and you'll be very, *very* sorry."

"But what are we going to *do*?" He whispered.

"Maybe we'll go to Sears and play TV Ping-Pong."

"The salesman's too mean."

"We'll wait till he's on his coffee break or something. Is Johnny up?"

"I'll wake him."

Roy loved to wake people. He had his own method, which he considered kind and considerate. He simply breathed on them until they opened their eyes. He hurried from the room, the legs of his jeans brushing together as he ran.

He went into the bedroom and leaned on the bed. It sank with the pressure of his elbows. He bent over Johnny.

Johnny stirred with irritation. "Get away from me," he said without opening his eyes.

"It's me—Roy."

"I know it's you, peanut butter breath," Johnny snarled. He turned over. "Now get off my bed."

"It's my bed too!"

Roy hesitated. He was disapponted. He remained with his elbows on the bed, staring at Johnny's back. A breeze blew in the window, and Roy glanced over at the billowing curtains. A heavy, sweet smell filled the room.

The Bowlwater plant, Roy thought. His frown disappeared. A slight smile came over his face.

To Roy, the Bowlwater plant was the most enormous bush in the world, something out of "Jack and the Beanstalk." Any plant that could produce such a strong, fascinating smell, a smell Roy associated with the Orient, *that* plant had to have leaves as big as bed sheets and flowers like tubas. No one had ever explained to Roy that the Bowlwater plant was a factory that made chemicals, and when the wind blew from the southwest, it brought the smell of chemicals with it.

Roy's ambition was to see the Bowlwater plant, climb on it, slide down the leaves, and later—when he got a piece of paper big enough—to draw a picture of it.

He looked at Johnny again. He said, "Want to smell the Bowlwater plant? Open your eyes and you can." He spoke in the voice he used in kindergarten when Miss Elizabeth said, "Let's use our *indoor* voices, boys and girls."

Johnny yanked the sheet up over his head. He flopped over, writhing with irritation.

Roy was irritated too. He abandoned his gentle methods. He said, "You better get up if you want to go with me and Retta." He stood up and waited, hands on hips.

"Where are you going?" Johnny asked without removing the sheet.

"We're going to Sears and play TV Ping-Pong."

"Go ahead."

"All right, we just will." He started from the room. "But don't blame me if *we* have a good time and *you* don't."

"Get out of here."

"I'm going. I just don't want you to blame me if—"

"Get *out!*"

Roy was discontent. Even the mysterious scent of the Bowlwater plant could not soothe him now. "He won't get up," he told Retta. He waited in the doorway, watching Retta hopefully.

Retta had always been his daytime mother. Even when his real mother was alive, it had been Retta who looked after him. He admired her most when she acted like the mothers he saw in grocery stores, mothers who shook their kids and said things like, "You touch another can, and I'll can *you!*" *That* was mothering.

He wanted Retta to put her maternal skills to use now. He wanted her to pull Johnny out of the bed by his ear. "You'll play Ping-Pong or I'll Ping-Pong *you!*"

Retta remained on the floor. She began to tear a coupon from the newspaper. "Hey, there's a merry-go-round at the mall. With this," she waved the coupon in the air, "and a sales slip from Murphy's you can ride free."

"But do we have a sales slip?" Roy took two steps into the room.

"We'll fish one out of the trash can, if we have to."

Roy's excitement rose. "Let's don't tell Johnny, all right? And when we get home you can say, 'Listen, you wouldn't get up when Roy called you,' and he'll say, 'I didn't know there was a merry-go-round,' and you can say—"

"Come on. The rain's stopping."

They walked out the door and paused on the top step. Roy inhaled deeply. "I smell the Bowlwater plant," he told Retta. Visions of the plant rose again in his mind, the trumpetlike blossoms blowing out odor like music. "Can you walk to the Bowlwater plant?" he asked.

"No, it's too far."

"Can you go on the bus?"

"I think so."

"Someday," he promised himself, "I'm going there."

Johnny lay in bed. He heard the front door slam, and he threw back the sheet as if he were going to get up and run after Roy and Retta. Instead he lay staring up at the ceiling.

He felt a deep resentment at Retta and Roy for going off without him. Even though he had said he didn't want to go, they should have begged him. The thought that if he hurried he could still catch them made him even angrier.

He got up slowly and walked into the living room. He could see Retta and Roy waiting at the edge of the porch. "I thought you'd gone," he said, drawing his mouth into a sneer.

Retta turned. "The rain's stopped. You want to

come to the mall with us? There's a merry-go-round."

"But we've only got *one* coupon," Roy said importantly. "So only one of us gets to ride and that's me, isn't that right, Retta?"

"We can get another coupon if—"

"Only *babies* ride on merry-go-rounds," Johnny said.

Roy's mouth fell open. He was stung by the insult. He turned to Retta. "That's not true, is it? He's just saying that, isn't he, because he doesn't have a coupon and I do?"

Johnny started into the kitchen. He was aware that Roy was probably making a face at him through the screen door but he did not turn around.

"We'll be back soon," Retta called.

"I don't care if you never come back," Johnny grumbled. He opened the refrigerator door, took out the milk, and drank directly from the carton, something Retta did not allow them to do. Then he walked into his father's room.

He looked down at his father. Shorty Anderson was lying on the bed in his underwear. There was a faint smile on his face.

"Dad?"

Shorty Anderson did not move. He was half asleep and he was dreaming about the new song he had written and recorded the week before. It was called "You're Fifty Pounds Too Much

Woman for Me." In his dream he was singing the chorus at the Grand Ole Opry. "When you get eatin' off your mind, I'll get cheatin' off of mine. I don't want no extry woman in my aaaaaaarms," he sang to himself.

"Dad?"

Shorty Anderson heard Johnny's voice, and the Grand Ole Opry began to fade away. He was not there on the stage in a red satin cowboy shirt with the lights picking up the glitter of the rhinestones. He was here in bed in his dirty underwear. He let the air out of his lungs in a long sigh.

"What's wrong?" he asked without opening his eyes. Usually he played a game when the kids came into his room in which he pretended to get their voices mixed up. Roy would become so agitated when his voice was mistaken for Retta's that he would pry his father's eyes open to prove his identity. Shorty Anderson wasn't up to games this morning.

"Nothing," Johnny said. "I was just wondering if you were going to get up."

"In a little bit."

Jonny continued to stand beside his father's bed. "Retta and Roy went to the mall."

"They did?" Shorty Anderson said without interest.

"Yes, they didn't want me." Despite Johnny's efforts to keep his voice normal, a tremor of self-pity ruined the sentence.

"They wanted you."

"They *didn't*. They *hate* me, and I hate *them*."

Shorty Anderson's eyes were still closed. He was thinking about his song again. He wanted a hit recording more than anything in the world. The closest he had ever come to success was with a song called "My Angel Went to Heaven in a DC-3," which he had written and recorded just after his wife died.

His wife, Mavis Lynn, had been a singer, too, and she had been killed in a plane crash on her way to a state fair in Kentucky. Shorty wrote the song the next night, and within a month it had risen to number thirty-seven on the country-western charts.

Shorty Anderson had been much in demand during that time, and he had had a black satin cowboy outfit made up for his appearances. Within another month the song went off the charts, and Shorty went back to wearing the reds and pinks and purples that he preferred. People still remembered the song, however, and every time he started singing it, there would be a little applause of recognition.

Watching "My Angel went to Heaven in a DC-3" move up the charts had made him happier than anything else in his life. In his opinion "You're Fifty Pounds Too Much Woman for Me" could go all the way.

Johnny noticed the faint smile on his father's face, the same smile that had been there when he first came into the bedroom.

"Dad!"

"What's wrong now?"

"You're going back to sleep. You aren't even listening to me."

"I'm listening. What's wrong?"

"*Nothing!*" He stamped heavily out of the room.

"Johnny!"

Johnny paused in the hall. "What do you want?" he asked in a dejected voice. He did not bother to turn around.

"Is there any coffee?"

"*Retta* drank it all," he said in a hard, accusing voice.

"Well, would you make some more?"

There was a long pause. "I guess," he said. Shoulders sagging, he went into the kitchen.

Behind him Shorty Anderson began to sing aloud. "If you get eatin' off of your mind, I'll get cheatin' off of mine. I don't want no extry woman in my aaaaaarms."

He sat up and swung his feet off the bed. They did not touch the floor. "Hey, Johnny-Oh! Make me a piece of toast while you're at it."

In the kitchen Johnny let his shoulders sag even more. With his mouth turned down as sad as a clown's, he reached for the instant coffee.

Roy was sitting at the kitchen table making men out of Pillsbury refrigerated dough. He had worked over them so long that they had a gray look. He was now rolling a piece of dough between both hands.

"This man's going to have a tail and it's going to be soooo long that you won't believe it."

The dough was hanging out the bottom of his hands, swinging back and forth.

"Well, don't make them too funny looking or Dad won't want to eat them." Retta glanced at him. "Roy, did you wash your hands before you started?"

"Yes, I washed my hands before I started," he said, imitating her tone and wagging his head from side to side.

With great care he attached the tail to the dough man and curled it upward. When the angle of the tail was perfect, he rubbed his hands proudly on his shirt.

"I get the one with the tail," he said.

He was still looking at his dough men with a fond, pleased smile when Johnny came into the kitchen. "Want to see what I'm making?" Roy asked.

"Nope."

"I'm making dough men."

"I'm not going to eat any of them. They're filthy." He crossed to where Retta was working at the stove. "What's for supper?"

"Spaghetti."

"You call what you make spaghetti?" Johnny asked. "It's nothing but tomato soup poured over noodles. Real spaghetti has meat in it and onions and a lot of other stuff."

Retta was never hurt by criticism of her cooking because she herself was always pleased with the results. She got a lot of her ideas from the school cafeteria and from Kraft television commercials.

"Where did you go?" Retta asked. She took a sip of soup to check the flavor, then turned to Johnny. "We came back to get you and you were gone. We found an extra coupon and—"

"*And,*" Roy broke in, wanting to tell the important part himself, "since you weren't there, I got your ride too." He patted his dough men happily.

He wished they wouldn't keep rising. "Now, stay down," he told them.

"I went out," Johnny said in a casual way.

"On *my* ride I got on a giraffe," Roy said, "and on *your* ride I got on an elephant."

Johnny remained at Retta's side. He wanted her to ask him exactly where he had been because he was eager to tell her.

She glanced around him. "Are those ready for the oven?" she asked Roy. "Have you now made every single one as dirty as possible?"

"Want to know where I went?" Johnny asked.

"They're *not* dirty," Roy said defensively. He gave each one an extra pat.

"They are too. They're gray."

"They're supposed to be that color, aren't you, you guys?" He leaned over them.

Retta said, "If you start kissing them, nobody's going to eat them."

"I wasn't going to kiss them," Roy lied.

In the pause that followed, Johnny said, "In case anybody is interested in what I did this afternoon, I went to the park and helped a boy set off rockets."

Roy looked up. His mouth fell open. He could not bear it when Johnny or Retta did something without him.

"*And* he also makes and flies model airplanes."

Roy's mouth formed an O. He was suddenly so jealous of Johnny's afternoon that as he straight-

ened, he pressed down on one of his dough men,
flattening it, and didn't even notice.

"He flies these airplanes with"—Johnny paused
to give importance to his next words—"radio controls." He now had both Retta's and Roy's attention. It was the most satisfying moment he had
known in a long time.

"And next time I go over there, he's going to
show me how to work the controls."

"Johnny," Roy wailed. "Why didn't you wait so
I could come too?"

Johnny shrugged. Smiling slightly, he turned
and started for the door. Even his walk was new
and important.

Roy had been kneeling on the kitchen chair so
that he could work more efficiently on his dough
men. Now he scrambled to the floor. "You'll let
me go next time, won't you, Johnny?" He followed
Johnny to the door. "You'll let me see the airplanes and the rockets, won't you?"

"Roy!" Retta's voice was suddenly sharp. "I
thought you wanted to watch your dough men
cook."

Roy paused in the doorway. His face was
twisted with indecision. Retta was putting his
dough men into the oven. He had intended to
press his face against the oven window and watch
the entire process, but now he abandoned the
idea. This was more important. He ran after
Johnny.

"Roy!" Retta called.

"Not now!"

Roy followed Johnny to the front porch. His excited pleas floated back through the house to where Retta stood at the stove. "Please take me, Johnny. And if you do, you can have the dough man with the tail."

Retta slammed the oven door shut and leaned against the stove. After a moment she began to push at the noodles with her spoon. The water boiled up around the edge of the pot. Retta felt as if her mind were boiling too.

Her change in mood had been seesaw-quick, so abrupt she couldn't understand it. A moment before she had been happy and satisfied with her day, contentedly letting Roy ruin the biscuits. Now, in some odd way, a balance had shifted and she was down.

She slapped the spoon against the noodles. She felt her bad spirits deepen.

This had nothing to do with the fact, she told herself, that Johnny had gone off and made a new friend. And it was not that Roy was out on the porch, begging and pleading, turning Johnny into some kind of supreme being just because he had a friend who made airplanes. It was that she wasn't appreciated, she decided abruptly. No one in the whole family appreciated her.

On the porch Roy was making one of his solemn promises. "I'll do anything in the whole world if you'll just take me with you."

Retta lifted a spoonful of noodles and let them

fall back into the water, not noticing that they were done. It seemed like a long time since Roy had begged *her* for anything other than food.

Shorty Anderson came into the kitchen doing a clog step. In his high-heeled boots he was two inches taller than his daughter; without them, an inch shorter.

"Supper ready, honey?"

"Almost," she said in an unhappy voice.

"Mmmmmm, looks good." Shorty Anderson was always cheerful in the evening when he was shaved, showered, dressed, and ready to go to his job at the Downtown Hoedown. He opened the oven door and glanced at Roy's dough men. "What are them things?"

"Dough men."

"Hooey! How many dads in this whole world are lucky enough to be having dough men for supper?" He danced around her.

She did not answer. Holding the pot with dish towels, she carried it to the sink. As she drained the water, she spilled a few drops of boiling water on her hand. Her throat swelled with tears.

Shorty Anderson looked over her shoulder. "I could eat that whole thing," he said.

"You always say that—"

"I mean it too."

"—and then you take about three bites and get up and leave."

"I have to, hon. Short people can't eat like other people."

Retta dumped the noodles in a bowl and poured the tomato soup over them. She stared at the dish disgustedly.

Shorty watched his daughter. He knew something was making her unhappy, just as he had known that morning that Johnny was unhappy. However, he never interfered. After all, he hadn't interfered with Johnny, and now, only eight hours later, Johnny was on the porch, problems solved, happy as a bug. Besides, if he asked Retta what was wrong, she might tell him.

"Dish me up a great big plateful," he said, hugging her. "Even if I can't eat it all, it makes me feel good to have a lot."

He sat at the table and began to spread paper napkins over his purple cowboy suit to protect it from spills. It took eight napkins. If he only used seven—he knew this from experience—he would spill something on that one uncovered spot.

"Boys," he called cheerfully, "soup's on!"

Retta slammed the bowl on the table. The noodles trembled. "It's not *soup!*" Retta said. The tears moved up from her throat to her eyes. "It's *spaghetti!*"

Shorty looked up in surprise from the safety of his paper napkins. "I know that, darling." He began to serve himself, taking more than he wanted. "Mmmmmmmm," he said as the steam reached his face. He tucked his napkins more securely around him and began to eat.

"And what's more, I need *seventeen dollars!*"

Retta said, leaning over the table toward her father.

"Well, hon, you can have it. I get paid tomorrow."

At that Retta burst into tears, ran from the kitchen into her room, and slammed the door. The door didn't catch and opened again, banging against the wall.

Through the open door she heard Shorty Anderson say, "Clean your plates now, boys. Retta's touchy tonight."

This time when she slammed the door, it stayed shut.

"Somebody's spying on us," Johnny said in a low voice. He reached across the water for Retta's arm.

It was the next night. The Anderson kids were in the Roberts's swimming pool. They were floating in the black inner tubes Retta had gotten, and they were holding on to each other so that they made a three-leaf clover in the center of the pool.

"Isn't this fun?" Retta had been saying as they turned in formation. "Don't you like your inner tubes?" She was trying to be especially bright and cheerful tonight to hide the fact that she was miserable. Also she wanted the evening to be a special success because Johnny hadn't wanted to come. "Aren't you having a good time, Johnny?"

"It's all right," Johnny had answered. He *was*

enjoying himself, but he was not going to let Retta know that. For the first time in his life he felt superior to his sister. He had *consented* to come—that was the way he thought of it.

He certainly was not going to jump up and down like Roy, screaming, "Inner tubes! Inner tubes!" After all, inner tubes were just old tires.

"Do you like your inner tube?" Retta had asked.

"I said it's all right."

Johnny could hardly believe that just getting a friend—even a fascinating friend who made rockets and airplanes—could make such a difference in his life.

Johnny had been seven years old when his mother died, and he had mourned her more than anyone. He would go into her closet and sit for hours hunched among her high-heeled boots, his face buried in the folds of her western outfits. He would dry his tears on her skirts before he crawled out.

After those first terrible weeks he had started clinging to the only person available—Retta. He had clung as tightly as a person in a storm, but now, somehow, he felt the storm was finally over. He felt he was stepping out into a world that actually welcomed him.

It was while he was enjoying his inner tube and this new security that he had noticed a figure by the garage. With his words, "Somebody's spying on us," the good feeling left him. He was, once again, a skinny kid in a patched inner tube, swimming illegally in the colonel's pool.

"Where?" Retta asked. She glanced up immediately at the darkened windows of the house. "I don't see anybody."

"Not there. There!" He pointed with one dripping arm to the garage.

"I still don't see anybody," Retta said.

There was a light that burned over the garage doors, casting a pale light on the driveway and bushes. Moths, drawn by the light, flitted around the bulb.

"Well, somebody was there a minute ago," Johnny said. "I saw them."

"Let's go home," Roy wailed. Being spied on, something he had never even thought about before, suddenly became the scariest thing there was.

"Oh, Johnny's just seeing things," Retta said. "Let's go around in our inner tubes again, want to? And this time—" She broke off because she, too, saw the figure moving behind the shrubbery. She paused in the water. Her long legs, which had been trailing behind her, sank like weights.

She had expected, had been prepared for the fact that some night the colonel might come striding out in his bathrobe. She had been prepared to shove her brothers to the opposite ladder and have them out of the pool and across the lawn in seconds.

But this strange figure, passing behind the bushes, this she had not been prepared for.

"Yes, I see him," Retta said in a low voice.

Roy struggled in his inner tube. "Where?" His round face was twisted with worry.

"He's gone now."

"I want to *see*!"

Retta turned and started swimming for the side of the pool. "I'm going to find out who it is," she said.

"Retta!" Roy grabbed for her but got only water. Kicking desperately, getting nowhere, he tried to move after her.

"I'm coming too," Johnny said.

Now Roy grabbed for Johnny, but Johnny was out of his reach too. "Wait for *me*!" he cried.

Retta was at the ladder. She pulled herself up and, dropping her inner tube, moved toward the garage. Johnny reached the ladder too. Roy struggled harder.

Retta and Johnny ran across the lawn. They paused at the garage and glanced around uneasily. Then they looked at each other.

Roy, fighting the water and the inner tube, reached the side of the pool at last. He flopped out like a seal.

"I want to go home," he wailed as he ran dripping across the lawn.

"Hush up! You want to wake the colonel?"

Roy was less afraid of the colonel than he was of the spy. "I don't care. I want to go home."

"Oh, all right!" Retta said. "I guess whoever it was is gone anyway." Now that she was at the garage, in the light, the desire to pursue the spy had left her. She, too, was ready to go home.

"I'll go back for the inner tubes. You two get the clothes," Retta said.

She was cold now, shivering. As she ran for the pool, she felt an unfamiliar weakness in her knees. She gathered the inner tubes and, holding them in both arms, ran to join her brothers.

Roy and Johnny were already running for the fence, their clothes clutched to their chests. Roy glanced back over his shoulder to make sure only Retta was behind him.

Roy had never enjoyed being scared the way some children did. He put his hands over his eyes during the scary parts of movies. He put his hands over his ears when Retta told that fearful story, "I'm on the first step. I'm on the second step. I'm on the third step." He could not bear that final "*Got you!*" Now that it seemed about to happen to him, he was moving the way he moved in his dreams—so slowly he could never get away.

He glanced back over his shoulder again. This time he stumbled over a bush and fell, dropping his Chubbie jeans in the darkness.

"Rettaaaaaa!" he wailed.

She was there instantly. She yanked him to his feet in one swift movement. "There." She swooped up his clothes. Holding the inner tubes awkwardly on one hip, she led him to the fence.

As they scrambled over, Retta glanced back at the garage.

The figure was there, watching as they ran away.

"Let's go!" Retta said.

"Don't bother me now," Retta said. She was pretending to watch television.

"But I want to know if we're going swimming again or if we're not," Roy persisted. He was worried. He wanted Retta to promise that they would never, ever go swimming again because he was afraid. All night in his dreams he had run without getting anywhere.

"Of course we're going again. No stupid spy is going to keep us from experiencing things."

"But there's some things people don't want to experience," Roy said earnestly. He was remembering not only the evening before at the swimming pool but a long painful story a boy in his kindergarten had once told during Show and Tell about having his tonsils out.

"Look," Retta said, straightening, "I'm not going to allow us to grow up ignorant."

"I *know* that."

Roy sighed. Retta was already a stricter teacher than Miss Elizabeth. Once Retta had slapped Johnny when he was reading aloud and pronounced island "*is*-land" for the third time. The worst thing Miss Elizabeth ever did was shake you by the arm.

"*Why* do we have to go swimming again though?" he asked. The thought of having to climb down into that cold, dark water while spies waited in the bushes made his voice tremble. He blinked back tears.

Retta gave Roy a serious look. "Listen, Roy, life's more than just school stuff."

"I *know* that."

"I mean, reading and arithmetic are important because you don't want to go to a fancy restaurant and count up the bill on your fingers, do you?"

"No."

"But other things count too." She was looking at him so sternly that he temporarily forgot his fear. "Swimming in a nice pool, for example—that's important. I mean, when you grow up and are invited to a nice pool, you want to know how to act, don't you?"

"Yes." Roy inhaled deeply. He imagined himself

as a grown man, floating in a pool in a black inner tube while onlookers admired his style. The frown on his face eased.

"And when we get to be grown-up and important," Retta's voice softened because this was one of her dreams, "when we're grown-up and have pools and nice houses and cars, what will we do?"

Roy struggled with his memory.

"We'll share our stuff."

Roy nodded. He imagined himself smiling from an upstairs window of his mansion while poor kids swam below in his pool. It was a pleasant picture. He said sincerely, "Retta, anybody who wants to swim in my pool can."

Retta smiled.

Encouraged, Roy went on. "I don't care how many kids get in my pool. They can even make the water run over and I won't care." He made a solemn promise. "Every kid in the world can get in my pool and I won't say one single word."

He paused. He was awed by the scope of his own generosity. In his mind kids from all nations jumped into his pool. The water rose. More kids arrived, many in native dress. They jumped in too. The water flooded his lawn.

Above, in his window, he smiled a benevolent smile. He made a papal gesture of welcome. "Jump right in, kids," he said grandly.

"I'm going out," Johnny said. He crossed between Retta and Roy. He could have gone out the back door, but he wanted to make sure they knew he was leaving.

Roy stopped smiling. "Where are you going?" he asked, taking one step forward.

"To see my friend."

"The one with the airplanes and rockets?"

"You got it."

"Johnny, can I go too?"

"No."

Roy paused. Then he said slyly, "I don't believe you've really got a friend!" This kind of thing always worked on him. If someone said to Roy, "I don't believe you've got a friend," he would say, "I do too, I'll show you!" He could see at once it wasn't going to work on Johnny.

Johnny sat down and began to retie his shoelaces. "I don't care whether you believe me or not." He got up, stretched, and started for the door.

"Why can't I come?" Roy whined. He followed Johnny to the door.

"Because."

"Why!"

"You really want to know? All right. You can't come because, one, you're a pest. Two, you whine. Three, you have peanut butter breath. Four, you touch things. Five, you act stupid."

"Tell me *really* why you don't want me to come," Roy persisted.

Johnny gave a snort of disgust and turned away. At the door he paused. He looked back at Roy, and then he glanced at Retta on the sofa.

"Oh, all right," he said. "You can come if you want to."

"Me? I can come?"

"Yes, if you don't act stupid and if you keep your hands off Arthur's stuff and if you don't act like a pest."

"I won't. I promise."

They went out the door without glancing back at Retta. She sat without moving. She could sense the excitement that joined them and fenced her out. She turned back to the television.

On the porch Roy was saying, "I'm going to act so intelligent you won't even believe it's me."

"If you act intelligent at all, I won't believe it's you. Now, keep up."

"Don't worry, I'll keep up. Look how fast I'm walking, Johnny." He ran down the steps.

Retta sighed. On the television a woman had just won a fur coat and a trip to Mexico and she was jumping up and down in the enormous coat.

Suddenly Retta got to her feet. She turned off the TV and walked to the door. Her brothers were at the end of the block, turning the corner. Then they moved out of sight.

Retta went out on the porch. She went down the steps slowly, idly, as if she weren't going anywhere important. But at the bottom of the steps she turned and started down the hill after her brothers.

She paused at the corner. Her brothers were crossing the street. Slowly, keeping a long distance between them, Retta followed.

Shorty Anderson was sitting in his corner of the living room with one leg slung over the arm of the chair. He had gotten up after Retta and the boys left, and he was now working out a new song on his guitar. His foot swung with the rhythm.

Ideas for songs were coming faster these days than he could write them down. This one, he hoped, would be the follow-up song for "You're Fifty Pounds Too Much Woman for Me." The title of this one was "You Used to Be Too Much Woman, but Now You Ain't Enough."

He was hunched over his guitar, strumming a chord, singing. "You used to be too much woman. You filled up lots of spaces."

He paused, his eyes looking up at the ceiling.

He strummed the chord again. "And now you lost your fifty pounds, but you lost it in all the wrong pla-a-a-ces."

He broke off as Retta came into the house. He gave her his not-now-I'm-composing-a-song look. She stood in the doorway watching him. Her face was as red as if she had gotten too much sun. She was breathing hard.

Shorty began to sing the chorus, playing to Retta as if she were an audience.

> *"Your hair's got thin, but your head's still thick.*
> *Your feet stayed big, but your legs are candle-*
> *   wicks.*
> *Your hips ain't round, and your ears weigh four-*
> *   teen pounds.*
> *Oh, you're not the right woman for meeeeee."*

He grinned at Retta. She pulled herself away from the doorway and started for the kitchen.

"How you like it?" Shorty called after her.

"Fine."

"Want to hear the second verse?"

No answer.

Undaunted, Shorty began to sing.

> *"Your teeth thinned down, but your lips swelled*
> *   out.*
> *Your nose got fat and your chin's a waterspout.*
> *Your cheeks they flap, and your eyelids overlap.*
> *Oh, you're not the right woman for meeeeee."*

Retta sat down at the table. The kitchen was big and old. The cabinets had old-timey glass doors that showed the unmatched dishes. The table was covered with oilcloth in which Roy had poked holes with his fork.

In the living room Shorty Anderson started over. He liked the verses, but he wasn't satisfied with the opening.

"You used to be too much woman," he sang. He paused, waiting for an inspiration. When none came, he started over. "You used to be too much woooooooman . . ."

Johnny came into the kitchen by the back door, and Retta glanced up. Johnny was walking in his new, important way. His hands were in his pockets. He made a point of not looking at Retta.

Behind him Roy was babbling about the afternoon. "I didn't really believe you about the airplane. I'm not kidding. I didn't really believe it was true!" His face, red with heat and joy, shone in the sunlight from the window.

Roy was happily amazed because, as of late, his world had been drying up like a raisin.

"I didn't believe it was true," Roy told the cabinets, the refrigerator.

Once Roy had believed anything was possible. For example, he had had high hopes of digging to China. He had envisioned going down through layers of earth and popping up in front of startled Chinese. He had drawn a picture of the event in kindergarten, of the world with a line right through the middle—his tunnel—and a bubble at the end—his head. He was getting ready to draw the startled Chinese when Miss Elizabeth took up the papers.

Once, too, he had thought he would fly, not in airplanes like other people, but by flapping his arms. There was a certain spot on his body that he would press and he would rise into the air as easily as a bird. As soon as he found that spot, he intended to fly straight to another planet.

But lately his world, once as magical and enchanting as a fairy tale, was becoming narrowed by rules and laws.

The sight of that yellow airplane in the sky had somehow given him back a faith in the world's possibilities. He had reeled with pleasure and grown dizzy from turning his face upward.

He had forgotten his promise to be intelligent, and Johnny had had to tell him to shut up twice and to get out of the way a dozen times. Still, the afternoon had been a great success.

Johnny moved through the kitchen, still walking in an important way. He opened the refrigerator door. Retta watched him with wary eyes. "Don't eat the hard-boiled eggs," she snapped. "That's supper."

Johnny did not bother to look closely. He was not really hungry. He just wanted to come in and let Retta hear Roy babbling about the afternoon. He wanted her to know the afternoon had been a bigger success than any she had planned.

He slammed the refrigerator door in disgust.
The bottles and jars rattled.

"We never have anything to eat around here,"
he complained. "Come on, Roy."

"Yeah, we never have anything to eat around
here."

The two of them went out the door, leaving
Retta alone at the table. Roy's voice saying, "I
really, honestly, and truly didn't believe it was
true!" floated back to her through the window.

Retta put her chin in her hands and slowly exhaled. She thought about the afternoon. It had the
long, unreal beat of a fever dream.

She had followed her brothers all the way to the
park, keeping a good distance away. And at the
park she had sat alone under a tree and looked
down the hill at the field where her brothers
waited.

Staring down at them with slitted eyes, she had
hoped, first, that their friend would not appear,
hoped even that there was no friend. But then he
came, a tall, skinny boy laden down with a yellow
airplane. Her bad feelings swelled. She began to
will misfortune upon them. She hoped the plane
would not start, then that it would crash into the
ground. She had felt like an evil witch made suddenly powerless to cause the trouble she wanted.

When it was obvious that the flight was suc-
cessful, Retta had gotten up and started for home.
Halfway there she began running, stumbling over
the sidewalk even though she knew every crack

and buckle. She had come into the house, flushed, out of breath, to find her father with his guitar. Her harsh look had continued, piercing Shorty Anderson in his red cowboy shirt. It seemed that all her life, at every vital moment, Shorty Anderson had been composing a song.

She had stood there, heart pounding so hard she couldn't hear the words he was singing. And she had suddenly felt as if she were seeing her father so clearly that her image of him might be damaged forever, the way one's eyes are damaged by looking directly at the sun.

She remembered the night after her mother died. Retta had come into the living room to be with her father. It was late, but Retta had not been asleep; indeed, she was so troubled she thought she would never sleep gain. She had drawn close to her father.

"You can stay in here," Shorty had told her, "but you have to be quiet."

"I will."

It was three o'clock in the morning, and Shorty was playing his guitar. Retta lay on the sofa, nightgown wrapped around her thin body, eyes on her father.

Shorty Anderson was bent over his guitar, intent. His voice rose, then fell. The phrase, "Yes, my angelllll went to heavennnnn in a D . . . C . . . three!" filtered through her unhappiness.

"Are you writing a song about Mama?"

He nodded without looking up. She turned her head away. That was her last memory of that night. But the unswallowed, unspoken pain of her mother's death stayed in her throat so long that sometimes she thought she would die of it.

Retta sat at the kitchen table without moving. She stared down at her hands. Everything was clear to her now. Her father's goal—becoming a star, achieving a place where his voice made people laugh and cry, his clothes made people stare, where his life itself became the daydreams of ordinary people—that goal was so powerful that everything else, even his family, became a mere interruption.

If I died, she thought, Shorty Anderson would just write a song about that too. She put her face in her hands and sighed. In the silent kitchen her sigh had the slow, dangerous sound of a snake's hiss.

The Anderson kids came out of the bushes slowly, shy even though they were in their new bathing suits. They glanced, not at the pool shimmering in the moonlight, but at the bushes and trees, the shadows where somebody might be hiding, spying on them.

"Do you see anybody, Retta?" Roy called quietly. He was standing close to the bushes. Out of habit he held up his bathing suit with one hand.

"No, I do not see anybody," Retta said firmly, "and that is because nobody is here."

She had had a hard time getting her brothers to come tonight. Roy was afraid to come, and admitted it, but Johnny had pretended he had better things to do.

"What?"

"Things!"

"Oh, both of you are *scared*. You make me sick."

"I'll show you who's scared!" Johnny had said then, throwing open the front door and going outside.

"Well, don't forget your bathing suit!"

And now here they were, moving so slowly across the lawn that they still had not left the shelter of the shrubbery. Retta felt as uneasy as her brothers. All the pleasure of swimming in the colonel's pool was gone, but she was determined not to let that stop her.

She glanced over her shoulder and saw that Roy had not moved. "Are you just going to stand there all night like the Pillsbury Doughboy?"

He shook his head. His eyes rolled fearfully to the garage. His plump toes curled down as if to clutch the grass and hold him in place.

"Come *on*," Retta said through her teeth. Her eyes shifted to Johnny. "And for someone who isn't *scared*, you certainly are sticking close to the bushes. You remind me of a weasel."

She looked at her brothers critically. For the first time she was struck by their physical shortcomings. The new bathing suits, she decided, made them look even worse. Johnny's was too big and Roy's too little, so that in their matching striped suits they accented each other's faults.

"All the trouble I went to getting those bathing suits and then you act like this!" Retta had spent that whole morning walking to the shopping center, picking out the suits, walking home.

"I wanted blue," Roy had whined as she pulled his out of the bag, and Retta had thrown the suit at him so hard he had put up his fat arms in defense.

"I don't know why I even bother with you!"

She frowned at them. She wanted to make them presentable, the way mothers change a child by tugging a collar, yanking a belt into place, smoothing hairs. It would, she decided, take a lot more than that to make these two presentable.

The intensity of her dislike for her brothers surprised her because she had never really hated anyone before. She thought she had. She thought she had hated her third grade music teacher who criticized her singing, and two girls in her homeroom who whispered about her clothes, and the neighbors who disapproved of her family. That, she saw now, was only mild dislike. This was hate.

"All right, stay there and rot, chickens!" she taunted. "*I'm* going swimming!"

She strode toward the swimming pool, taking big steps, swinging her arms boldly. She did not glance behind her because she was certain Johnny would follow.

"I'll show you who's chicken!" Johnny yelled suddenly.

Retta turned.

Johnny came running toward her. He passed her so quickly that she felt the breeze. His skinny arms pumped. His legs, long pale sticks in the moonlight, scissored over the ground.

"Johnneeee!" she warned. He did not even glance in her direction.

Retta stepped back. Her hands rose to her chest, covering the flowers on her new bathing suit. Her mouth was slightly open.

Johnny reached the edge of the patio. He didn't pause. He headed for the forbidden diving board. "Even *I* can't go off the board," Retta had told them. "Even *I* would splash."

"Johnneeeee!" Retta's voice rose with her concern.

Johnny was on the diving board now. He ran to the end, bounced once, and then threw himself into the air, making ball of his body. As he hit the water, the splash seemed to cause sound waves in the air. It was like an explosion, loud enough to mark the end of something. In the after-silence, water sprayed lightly onto the patio tiles.

"Oh, Johnny," Retta said in a flat voice. She stood like a lawn statue with her arms over her chest. With the moonlight upon her, she was as pale as marble.

There was a moment of calm. Moonlit shadows flickered over the lawn. A bird called.

Then everything happened at once. A light went on upstairs in the house. A solid square of light shone on the pool. In this square of light

Johnny's head bobbed to the surface. He struggled to the side of the pool.

The colonel was at the window now. He peered down through his Venetian blinds at the pool. He turned abruptly and disappeared from view.

Retta ran forward a few steps. "Johnny!" His head appeared over the side. He pulled himself out and flopped onto his stomach. He got to his feet and began to run.

The downstairs lights went on in the house. The patio lights went on. The pool lights. Johnny was spotlighted as he scrambled to his feet in his new red-striped bathing suit.

He slipped on the wet tile, went down on one knee, and got to his feet. He was running again, heading for the bushes.

The door to the house was flung open. The colonel stood in the doorway in his shorty pajamas, glaring out into the brightly lit yard. He put one hand up to shield his eyes.

"Who's out there?" he yelled. His voice boomed through the silent night. "What's going on?"

Johnny was on the grass now, zigzagging across the lawn like a soldier trying to avoid gunfire. He passed Retta, spraying her with water.

With a start, Retta joined him. She scooped up her clothes and Roy's and grabbed Roy's arm as she came out of the bushes. The three of them ran for the fence.

"Stop! This is trespassing!" the colonel shouted.

He was striding across the patio now. Outrage made him look like a military man even in his shorty pajamas.

"Stop or I'll call the police!"

Roy, Johnny, and Retta were at the fence now, crawling over. Even Roy with his short legs was moving like an athlete. They dropped into the ditch and ran for the road. The only sound was Roy's hard breathing.

"Keep running," Retta gasped.

She was dividing up the clothes as they ran, handing Roy his T-shirt, pulling on her own blouse. She broke stride to put one leg into her jeans, then the other.

Beside her, Roy refused to pause even to put on his pants. As a concession to modesty, he held his pants in front of his bathing suit so that anyone who saw him from the front would think he was fully clothed.

At last they reached the house, entered, and slammed the door behind them. Retta threw the lock into place, something she had never done before. She leaned against the door, weak with the narrowness of their escape.

She looked at Johnny, who had sunk onto the sofa. His clothes were in a bundle on his lap. His skinny chest rose and fell as he tried to get his breath.

"Why did you do that?" Retta asked.

"Yeah, Johnny," Roy gasped, "we could have been arrested."

Johnny looked up at them. Water ran down his forehead from his dripping hair. He wrapped his clothes tighter and put them under his arm like a football.

"Now who's chicken?" he said.

Roy was connecting dots in a puzzle book he had given Johnny for his birthday.

"You're going to ruin Johnny's book," Retta said. She was sitting on the sofa watching him critically.

"I am not."

He connected the next two dots with special care and drew back to view his work. He nodded his approval.

"You don't know your numbers," Retta went on. "How can you connect *numbered* dots when you don't know your numbers?"

"This happens to be a picture of a pony and I *do* know ponies. I rode on one one time."

He bent over the book again. He loved to connect dots. He considered becoming a dot connector when he grew up. He liked the thought of himself at a desk, connecting dots while his secretary sharpened pencils.

"That's no pony," Retta said in a disgusted voice.

Roy jerked the book up and hid the half-finished picture against his chest. "It is too."

"It's a *zebra*. You're supposed to be going up and down making stripes instead of plodding on around!"

Retta got up and went to the kitchen. When she was gone, Roy lowered his book and looked critically at his picture.

"I was *going* to make the stripes," he explained to the empty doorway, "only I was doing the outside dots *first*, so *there!*"

Retta did not answer.

"You think you know everything."

He connected two dots, one at the top of the zebra, one at the bottom. He regarded his work with pleasure.

"Well, you *don't!*"

He heard the sound of water in the kitchen. He began nodding his head for emphasis. "You don't even know who was spying on us night before last."

The water stopped running. There was a silence in the kitchen and in the living room.

Roy realized what he had said. His fingers, fat

as sausages, flattened his mouth. His eyes rolled to Retta as she appeared in the doorway.

"What did you say?" she asked in a quiet voice.

"Nothing."

Retta crossed the room as quickly as the mothers in the supermarket rushed to keep their children from toppling toilet paper pyramids.

"I want to know what you said."

"Nothing!"

Her fingers closed around his arm. She was the grocery store mother he had admired and feared and loved to see grabbing other children. He found himself doing exactly what those other children did—twisting to get free. "You're hurting me," he whined.

"Do you know who was spying on us?"

"Ow!"

"Roy!"

"I can't think when you squeeze my arm like that."

"All right!" She released him. "Your fat arm is free. Now think."

He rubbed his arm. He couldn't even remember the question. Tears of self-pity welled in his eyes.

"Do you know who was spying on us?" Retta asked in an unnaturally calm voice.

"Yes."

"Who?"

Roy's arm still bore her fingerprint marks. He regarded his arm closely. "Look," he accused, "you *squeezed*."

"And I'm squeezing again if you don't tell me right this minute." She reached toward him.

"All right!" He drew back. He hesitated. He had promised Johnny he would not tell Retta, and he now weighed Retta's anger against Johnny's. The deciding factor was that Retta was here, threatening pain now.

"It was Arthur," he confessed quickly.

"What? Who's Arthur?"

"Johnny's friend—you know, with the airplane?"

"*He* was spying on us?"

"Yes, but he wasn't doing it to be mean. Johnny said so. Arthur happened to see us walking down the street one night with our inner tubes and he wondered where we were going. He just moved here, see, like us, and he didn't know where people swam. That was all. He and Johnny laughed about it later. Johnny said not to tell you because he wanted you to be worried."

"*Did* he?"

Retta was cold now. She seemed suddenly taller, an adult. Roy looked up at her. He hesitated for a moment. Then he surprised himself by saying, "Anyway, *you* spied on *us*."

The tone of his voice made it an accusation, and Retta looked down at him in surprise. "What?"

"You did too spy on us. At the park."

"I did not *spy*."

Johnny said you did. He saw you. He said you were sitting under a tree and as soon as we finished flying the plane, you got up and ran home and sat down at the table so we'd think you'd been there the whole time."

Retta straightened. She tried to regain the powerful, adult feeling she had had only a moment before, but the room seemed to have tilted and left her off-balance. "That was different," she said.

"No." Roy shook his head back and forth. "It was the same."

"It was different," she explained, "because I was looking after you guys, making sure you were all right."

"You were spying," Roy said.

"If you are so stupid that you can't tell the difference between looking after someone and spying on someone—well, you're just hopeless, that's all."

She turned abruptly and strode into the kitchen. There was an explosion of sounds. Water rushed into the sink. Pots rattled. Dishes spun on the table. The refrigerator door slammed.

"Spying is spying," Roy said wisely.

He went back to his book. With great care he connected the dots on the zebra's tail. He had been saving that till last, like dessert. As an added personal touch he drew seven hairs on the end of the zebra's tail. He was so pleased with this original touch that he wanted to rush out the door and show it to the world.

Head shaking with admiration, he paid the picture his highest compliment.

"You," he said, "should be put in a frame."

Retta sat on the back steps with her arms over her knees. She lifted her head idly and looked at the house behind theirs. A face at one window moved out of sight. Retta closed her eyes.

She had felt isolated ever since her family moved to this neighborhood. It was a neighborhood of old people, and Retta knew that none of them approved of the Anderson family. When Shorty Anderson went out at night, rhinestones gleaming, high-gloss boots clicking on the pavement, yelling, "Be good!" to his children on the porch, Retta saw the older women on their porches look at each other and shake their heads. They also disapproved, Retta knew, of the Anderson children who "ran loose at night like dogs."

If we still lived in our old neighborhood, Retta thought, where we had friends . . .

"Well, what are you doing out here all by yourself?" a voice asked behind her.

Retta glanced over her shoulder at the screen door. "Oh, hi, Brendelle." Brendelle was Shorty Anderson's girl friend.

"I just stopped by and Shorty invited me to stay for supper. You going to have enough?"

"We're just having grilled peanut butter sandwiches," Retta said without interest.

"Oh, listen, grill me two. I love them things."

Brendelle stepped onto the porch and let the screen door slam behind her. She sat on the steps beside Retta. She stuck out her left foot and pulled up the leg of her pants. "Look at that," she said. "I'm supposed to clog tonight at the Downtown Hoedown and my ankle is swollen up like a football."

"What happened?" Retta asked, still looking across the fence.

"I was getting in the car over at Foodland and this new boy was carrying out my groceries and he puts the groceries in the backseat and then he goes, 'Have a nice day, ma'am,' and slams the front door right on my leg. My leg was sticking out, you know, like it does when you're getting in the car. I wanted to hit him over the head. I mean, honey, I got to clog tonight and you got to have two good legs to clog. You think anybody's going to notice?"

"No."

Brendelle turned her leg and looked at it critically from another angle. "Is it getting purple on this side or is that my imagination?"

"It is purple."

"Maybe I can wear some real dark hose."

Brendelle lowered her foot and her pants leg. " 'Have a nice day, ma'am.' Bang!" She re-created the incident, imitating the carry-out boy perfectly. "And the bag of groceries wasn't any bigger than that." She sighed. "The only reason he wanted to help me was because behind me was a woman with great big bags of flour and potatoes, and he didn't want to help her." She straightened. "Hey, where are the boys? I want to see them."

"I don't know where they are."

"They'll be here for supper, won't they?"

"I guess."

"Why, Retta, I thought you ran herd on those boys. I thought you knew where they were every minute of every day."

"I used to. They got a new friend, though, and I never know where they are now."

"Well, that's nice—the boys having a new friend. All three of you ought to get out more."

"His name is *Arthur*." Retta made the name sound as ugly as possible.

"I used to know an Arthur," Brendelle remembered. "Arthur Lee Gribble."

"I hope he was better than this Arthur."

"Well, he wasn't. He asked me out one time and

I didn't want to go because he was bald and in those days I went for looks. Well, he wasn't *real* bald," she conceded, "but he had to part his hair low on the side and comb it over the top of his head to hide his bald spot, and the least little wind would ruin it."

Brendelle shifted as if trying to get comfortable on the wooden steps. "Anyway I didn't want to go out with him but finally I ran out of excuses and said, 'Oh, all right. Pick me up at eight o'clock.' I got all dressed up and I sat and waited and, would you believe it, he never showed up?"

"But if you didn't want to go out with him, why wouldn't you be glad he didn't show?"

"Because it don't work that way. No matter how much you don't want to go out with *them*, you want them to want to go out with *you*."

"I wouldn't."

"Later I saw Arthur Lee Gribble on the street and he goes, 'Don't I know you from somewhere?' and I go, 'No, I never forget a bald head.' " She straightened. "Hey, this Arthur—the boys' new friend—he's not nice?"

"I don't know. He spied on us once, I know that," Retta said.

"Spied on you?"

"Yes, while we were swimming."

"Where was you swimming at?"

Retta looked up at the pale summer sky. "Oh, nowhere," she said casually.

"Come on, I'd really like to know. I mean, if

you got friends with a private swimming pool, don't keep it to yourself."

"I don't have any friends with a swimming pool."

"That makes two of us."

Shorty Anderson opened the door behind them. He was dressed in his red cowboy suit with white satin cactus plants on the yoke. "Is this girl talk," he asked, "or can anybody jump in?"

"I was just telling Retta that I used to go for looks in a man," Brendelle said, grinning slyly, "but now I just go out with any old ugly thing that asks me."

"I'll pass the word along," he said, "if I run into any old ugly things." He nudged her in the back with his knee, and she got to her feet. She stretched.

"I—" She broke off as she saw Roy coming onto the porch. "Well, look who's here. Come here, Roy, I haven't hugged you in two weeks."

Roy came willingly. He loved to be hugged. Brendelle was the best hugger he had ever known because she put a lot of extras into her hugs. She swayed and patted him and scrubbed his hair and pretended to spank him. Then, just when he thought she was through, she would say, "One more time!" and start all over again.

"And where's Johnny?" she said. "I want to hug him too." She glanced over her shoulder at Shorty. "Way I'm acting, a person would think I'm half starved for masculine affection." She grinned. "Johnny, where are you?"

She had a hard time with Johnny because he didn't like to be touched. Sometimes Brendelle had to chase him for five minutes before she caught him. And then he would stand as stiff as an oar in her arms, hands at his sides, eyes closed tight.

Brendelle saw Johnny in the doorway. "I can't chase you tonight," she called. "A carry-out boy at Foodland crippled me. Look at that."

She held out her discolored ankle. Johnny hesitated for a moment and then came forward dutifully. Hands stiff at his sides, he walked into her arms.

She had both of the boys now. She hugged them together. It was as if she were trying, by squeezing them with all her might, to make the three of them into one huge, complicated package.

Johnny suffered the embrace with his eyes shut. Roy swayed with Brendelle, taking advantage of every aspect of the hug.

"I'll start the sandwiches," Retta said. She passed the three huggers, turning sideways so as not to disturb them. She went around her father in the same careful way. "Excuse me," she said.

"Put lots of peanut butter on my sandwich," Brendelle called happily. She grinned down at Roy and Johnny. "And put lots of oleo on the grill. I love goo."

She bent and kissed the top of Roy's head. "And so does Roy." She smoothed his hair back from his forehead so she could kiss his brow. "He wants the same thing, don't you, Roy? Lots of goo."

Roy lifted his head. His face shone. His answer had the earnest ring of a marriage vow.

"I do," he said.

"If you want to see Arthur, now's your chance," Roy sang at the window.

Retta glanced up from the television set. She had been watching television all day, but she didn't really know what she was seeing. The soap operas, the game shows, passed like one long, boring dream before her eyes. "What did you say?"

"Arthur's in our yard, so if you want to see what he looks like up close, you can."

"No."

"I had to come in the house," he said, his voice losing its happy lilt. "Arthur and Johnny were talking about something *secret*."

Roy stood at the window with his hands in his pockets. He was hurt. He hated to be left out.

Once in kindergarten he'd accidentally colored his George Washington face mask green and had not been allowed to march in the Parade of Presidents with the other kids. He had waited in the classroom with Miss Penny, weeping with the pain of exile, vowing never to be left out of anything again.

He glanced at Retta. He sensed that she really wanted to see Arthur up close but didn't want to admit it. Out of kindness he began to describe Arthur to her.

"Well, he's got on blue jeans with a patch in the back and a yellow T-shirt. There's writing on the shirt, but I can't read it. There's a Band-Aid on his elbow and a watch on his arm. He's got a—"

"Will you shut up? I am trying to watch television."

"That show's no good. It doesn't even have good commercials." Roy believed the quality of TV shows could be judged by the commercials. The most boring programs had commercials for false teeth glue and toilet paper.

"I'm not watching the commercials," Retta said, giving him a cool nod. "I'm watching the program."

Roy glanced out the window. "Arthur's leaving now," he reported. "He's walking down the sidewalk."

"Good."

"He's pausing, scratching his head, he's turning,

he's—" Suddenly he broke off. He drew in a long,
shuddering breath. "I smell the Bowlwater plant,"
he said happily.

"Maybe you smell *Arthur,*" Retta replied, making an ugly face as she said the name. She did not
take her eyes from the television set.

"No, it's the Bowlwater plant. I'd know that
smell anywhere."

In his mind the plant was growing, reaching for
the sky, shading the country side with its huge
leaves. The enormous flowers were swelling on
stems thicker than his arms and sending out their
magical fragrance, today, luckily, in his direction.

"I wish they'd close that plant down," Retta
said suddenly.

Roy looked at her. He was as astonished as if
she had proposed doing away with the Atlantic
Ocean. "They would never do that."

"They should."

"Anyway, why did you say *close* it down?" he
asked, puzzled. "You can *chop* down a plant,
maybe, or pull it up, but you can't *close down* a
plant."

Retta turned her eyes from the television. She
looked interested in Roy for the first time. "What
do you think the Bowlwater plant is?"

"A plant."

"What kind of plant?" she quizzed.

"A big plant." He was careful not to commit himself. Sometimes he got trapped that way and people laughed at him.

"Well, you got it," Retta said. "That's what it is—a big ugly plant."

"It's not ugly."

"Have you seen it?"

"In my mind," he said with a dignified nod. Roy felt as if he were moving toward something unpleasant. He felt himself on the edge of a step— one slip and he would descend into a world that was even less magical than it already was. He willed himself not to look down, willed the Bowl-water plant to be as he imagined.

"Somebody told me they make army chemicals there," Retta went on in a conversational tone. "That's chemicals that kill people and leave the cars and buildings so that the army can use them."

Roy didn't hear her. He had closed his mind. He was now interested only in what was happening in the yard.

"Arthur is leaving again," he said. "This time he's really going." Roy moved to the door and was waiting when Johnny stepped onto the porch. "What was so secret?" Roy asked.

"Nothing."

Johnny crossed the room, taking his time. He plopped down in his father's chair and slung one leg over the arm as his father did.

"If it wasn't secret, then why couldn't I hear it?"

"Don't bug me," Johnny said.

There was a silence. Retta tried to concentrate

on her television program, but she felt herself being drawn into her brothers' conflict. She looked at Johnny.

"I know you and Arthur are going to do something," Roy was saying, "and I want to know what it is."

"It's none of your business."

"I want to *know*! Are you going to fly the airplane or are you going to shoot the rockets?"

"Neither."

"Then what *are* you going to do?"

Retta said, "Don't beg him. That's exactly what he wants you to do."

"I do not," Johnny said. He sat up straight in his father's oversize chair. "What makes you think I want to be begged?"

"Because you're sitting there like the king of Arabia with that I-know-something-you-don't-know sneer on your face. You're disgusting."

"You're the one that's disgusting. You can't stand it, can you, that I have a friend and you don't?"

Retta stared at him as if he were an ugly, offensive stranger.

He got up slowly and walked toward the hall. At the doorway he paused and looked back at Retta and Roy. "I'll tell you one thing," he said, "whatever I'm going to do I'm going to do it without the two of you." He disappeared into his room.

Roy hit his fist against his leg. "I *knew* they were doing something secret." He turned to Retta. He sensed her helplessness, but he had nowhere else to turn. "Retta, make him tell me!"

Retta looked at the empty doorway. "I can't seem to make him do anything anymore," she said.

Roy rarely played with his food because he was always in a hurry to eat it. The one exception was mashed potatoes. Tonight he was making a volcano of his potatoes, smoothing the sides up to a pool of melted margarine in the middle.

A trickle of margarine ran down one side, and he quickly repaired the damage. He wished they were having green beans so he could plant trees on the side of his volcano—that way the eruption would be more dramatic. But tonight Retta had fixed only one thing—mashed potatoes.

The volcano was almost as tall as his cup of milk now, a really spectacular display. "Look," he said to Retta and Johnny.

He waited until he had their attention. Then,

making sound effects with his mouth, he erupted the volcano, sending margarine spilling down the sides, creating destruction on one side and then the other until the entire volcano was a flat mess of potatoes that covered his entire plate.

Satisfied at last, he picked up his spoon and began to eat. "Want me to make something out of your potatoes, Retta?" he asked.

"No."

"I can make anything—boats, rivers, planets—"

"No."

"I won't make anything for *Johnny* because he won't tell me the secret."

"Good," Johnny said.

Johnny and Retta were not eating. Neither was hungry. Johnny was too excited to eat because he and Arthur were going on a secret mission that night. Retta was too suspicious to eat. She knew Johnny was up to something—she could tell from the nervous energy that caused him to dig at his food, shift in his chair, pull at his clothes, and dig at his food again.

She watched Johnny with eyes sharp enough to penetrate his thoughts.

"Quit staring at me," he said finally.

"I'm not staring."

"You are too."

She looked down at her plate and shifted her potatoes with her fork. She lifted the fork and sipped the potatoes on it as if she were taking medicine. Her eyes rolled to Johnny.

"You're staring at me *again*!" he accused.

"Well, you're staring at me too!"

"All right, everybody," Shorty Anderson said, coming into the room with a square-dance step. "Everybody can stare at me!" He had on his hot-pink velour outfit with the rhinestone lapels, his favorite. He danced around the table in his matching leather boots.

"Supper's cold," Retta said.

"I don't believe I'll have anything, honey. I'll just get something at the Hoedown. Looks mighty good though." Shorty never took chances eating in his pink suit. It cost twenty-two dollars to have it cleaned.

"We had mashed potatoes," Roy said, "and I made a volcano."

"I used to do that when my mama wasn't looking," Shorty Anderson said. "But my mama wouldn't let us play with our food. That's the only bad thing I can say about her." He put one hand on Retta's shoulder. "You're lucky to have a sweet sister who lets you do what you want."

"Oh, Dad," Retta said through her teeth.

"Well, they are." He turned away. "You kids behave yourselves now."

"We will," Roy called happily.

Retta, Roy, and Johnny continued to sit at the table after their father left, even though they had finished eating. Retta kept her eyes down, but her thoughts were on Johnny. He's slipping out tonight, she said to herself.

Finally Johnny broke the silence. He stood up, stretching. "Well, I'm tired. I'm going to bed."

"It's only eight o'clock," Retta said.

"So—I'm tired. All right?"

As Johnny left the room, Retta looked up, eyes burning. She watched him until he disappeared into the hall. Then she got up and began to wash the dishes. Over the hot, steaming water, her face was set.

They all went to bed early. Roy fell asleep quickly, but Retta and Johnny lay wide awake, eyes staring at the ceiling. From time to time Johnny smiled slightly in anticipation, but Retta's face remained hard, unyielding.

She knew the exact moment when Johnny got out of bed because she heard the creak of his bed springs. She lay without moving, eyes shut, while Johnny slipped out of his room and into the hall.

Johnny paused in the doorway of Retta's room. He wanted to make sure Retta was asleep. If she stirred, he was going to pretend he was on his way to the bathroom. She did not move. Breathing a sigh of relief, Johnny moved quietly into the living room.

Johnny had always felt that the one thing he was really good at was not being noticed. Indeed, he sometimes thought he must be invisible. One day last fall, in school, his teacher, Miss Lipscomb, was passing out papers, matching pupils to papers, and then paused with one paper left in her hand.

"Johnny Anderson?" she had said. She had looked as puzzled as if the name were foreign. He raised his hand.

"Are you new?"

"No'm."

School had been going on for six weeks. He had not been absent a single day. Miss Lipscomb had shaken her head, smiling at herself. "Well, Johnny Anderson, you and I are going to have to get better acquainted."

"Yes'm," he had said, shifting so that he was, once again, hidden by the boy in front of him. In the spring, when he moved away, she said, "I really don't feel like I got to know you at all."

"No'm," he answered.

Now Johnny walked across the living room, opened the screen door, eased it shut, and went onto the porch. Leaning against the banister, he put on his shoes.

Inside the house Retta was getting out of bed. She was already dressed in her jeans and shirt, and she slipped noiselessly into the hall. She waited a moment in the darkness until she heard Johnny going down the steps.

As he turned onto the sidewalk, he began to pick up speed. Retta moved quickly onto the porch. She went down the steps and stood in the shadow of an elm tree. It was eleven o'clock, and the moon was full and bright, weaving in and out of the clouds.

Down the street, her brother was at the corner.

A car passed on Hunter Street and Johnny waited, then crossed quickly and broke into a run.

Retta glanced right and left to see if any snoopy neighbors were watching. All the houses on the street were dark. Keeping to the shadows, Retta moved quickly after Johnny.

Roy woke up and knew instantly that he was in bed alone. His side of the mattress was lower than usual. He flipped over and said, "Johnny?"

In the light from the living room he saw that the other half of the bed was empty.

"Johnny!"

He got up. He hated to be alone and he sensed that Johnny had not just gone to the bathroom or the kitchen. He stumbled into the hall, eyes alert, mouth worried, body still clumsy with sleep.

He staggered into Retta's room and turned on the light. When he saw that her bed was empty, too, he began to yell for either of them. "Retta! Johnny! Rettaaaaa!"

There was, as he had feared, no answer. He

went out onto the porch and sat down on the steps. He began to cry.

"Why did they leave me?" he asked mournfully. "People shouldn't go around leaving people."

He paused to wipe his tears on his pajama top. "I wouldn't have left them."

Each statement made him feel worse. He began to cry harder. "Next time I'm going to leave them and show them how it feels."

Even the thought of this just punishment did not cheer him. He could not bring into focus the picture of Retta and Johnny sitting on the steps, weeping, while he went off to some good time.

His tears came faster. Being left behind was a terrible feeling. He had always had a special feeling for anyone left behind. The night before, he had seen a television program where the pioneer family left their old dog behind while they went west. He had wept real tears for that dog.

Later in the show the dog followed the family and saved them from a surprise Indian attack by barking. "I don't care how many Indians attack Retta and Johnny," he said wetly, feeling a closer bond with the pioneer dog, "I won't let out one single bark."

The thought of Retta and Johnny going down under Indian attack while he waited in the bushes, lips sealed, was pleasant, but it didn't make him feel any better. He continued to weep quietly in the moonlight.

Suddenly he sat erect. He remembered that Johnny and Arthur had had some kind of secret. He licked at a tear on his cheek. He tasted the salt. And Retta had to be in on the secret, too, he thought. Everybody was in on it but him.

"They've gone swimming," he said abruptly.

He remembered that Retta had told him they could never go to the colonel's again, but that was probably just to throw him off the track. He got to his feet. The tears were drying on his cheeks. He went slowly down the steps.

As he stood on the last step, scarcely breathing, a wonderful plan came to him. He would sneak up to the colonel's house and spy on Retta and Johnny and Arthur. He was, it seemed to him, the only one who had not done any spying. They would see him in the shadows, he went on, and be terrified. He would feel no mercy. Abruptly he strode down the sidewalk in his striped pajamas.

At the edge of the street he stopped, struck dumb with an even better idea. When he got to the colonel's and saw that Johnny and Retta and Arthur were in the pool, he would run forward, whooping and yelling as Johnny had done, and dive in with them.

The picture of Johnny running across the lawn, not caring about anything or anybody, had impressed him deeply. It had seemed the kind of grown-up thing that he himself had never been able to do. If he lived to be a hundred, he would never feel more awe and respect for anyone than he had for Johnny as he launched himself off the diving board in that perfect cannonball.

The brilliance of his own plan washed over him. Arthur and Johnny and Retta would be in the pool, swimming quietly, trying not to splash. They would hear the sound of running. They would look up, mouths open, as he dashed forward. Before they knew what had happened, he would be launched off the diving board in the same fearless cannonball.

He hurried down the sidewalk. He no longer felt the twigs and stones beneath his bare feet.

"Ro-oooooy," Retta would say. He could hear her in his mind. He mimicked her as he walked, wagging his head from side to side. "Ro-ooooy!"

And Arthur—Arthur would be especially impressed because Arthur would not know he was copying something Johnny had done.

The pleasant dream continued. Retta would herd them all out of the swimming pool, and the four of them would run across the lawn, bonded together in their escape. Behind them the lights would be coming on in the colonel's house.

"Faster!" He would call back to the others. He himself would be in the lead at this point. "Come *on!*" The thought of being in the lead for the first time in his life made him shudder with pleasure.

The colonel's house appeared in the distance, big and white in the trees. Roy began to walk slower. He moved closer to the fence. There was a little smile on his face. His heart was beating so hard that he put his hand over his chest to make swallowing easier.

He climbed the fence by the trees as Retta had taught him to do. Overhead, the moon was hidden by a cloud, and he waited in the darkness, so tense and expectant that his knees were trembling. He swallowed again.

Bending, he began to creep toward the pool, a short stooped figure in wrinkled pajamas. He paused, lifted his head. He could not see what was happening in the pool, but he could hear the faint sound of splashing.

Still stooping, he ran forward. He crossed the clearing and paused by an azalea bush. He peered through the foliage with one hand over his eyes.

They *were* in the pool. He could hear them swimming. He straightened and drew in his breath. He moved his feet back and forth on the lawn, like a cartoon character getting ready to run.

Surprise is everything, he told himself. It's *got* to be a surprise. He leaped out from behind the bush and started running for the pool.

Runing across the lawn was wonderful. He felt powerful for the first time in his life. He didn't care about anything or anybody. He surprised himself by leaping up and letting out a whoop of joy.

He crossed the tiled patio, taking smaller steps now. He didn't want to slip. He headed for the diving board. He had a rush of panic as he ran to the end—he had never even been on a diving board before—but by taking tiny steps he managed not to fall off the side. His excitement carried him to the end of the board.

He had intended to bounce at least once, but he didn't have time. He fell immediately, curled forward like a shrimp. He hit the cold water and sank.

Roy came up struggling. He sputtered and reached out for Retta. In the excitement of his plan he had forgotten the crucial fact that he did not know how to swim. "Retta," he gasped. He choked and went under again.

Water went up his nose. He struggled for the surface, pulling desperately. He fell as if he were at the bottom of the sea and would never reach air. He bobbed up. He screamed Retta's name, choked, and went under again.

Suddenly he felt an arm grab him and pull him to the surface. He gasped for air. He turned blindly, wrapped himself around the arm, and crawled up to clutch the attached shoulder. He gagged on the water he had swallowed and held on tighter.

He felt himself being drawn to the side of the pool. He was lifted out and stretched out on the patio tiles. He was shivering violently. He gagged and began to cry.

"Retta!" He clutched the empty air, wanting her to hold him again. "Retta, I almost drowned!"

He looked up through his tears and saw that it was not Retta standing over him. He wiped the water from his eyes and saw the stern face of the colonel.

"Where's Retta?" Roy asked. His voice quivered on the night air like a bird's.

"Who is Retta?" the colonel asked.

And Roy turned over and gagged so hard that he lost not only the swimming pool water he had swallowed, but his mashed potato volcano as well.

Retta had been following her brother for four blocks. Her eyes were as intent as an eagle's on its prey.

She was breathing deeply, but she did not smell the scent of night flowers in the air. She was filled with the satisfaction that came from doing right. She was, at last, the mother she should have been all along—strong and purposeful. And it was not easy these days, she told herself, to be a strong and purposeful mother.

She lost Johnny as he went around the corner and she felt a quick anxiety. She walked faster. When she caught sight of him again, hands in his pockets, head up, she let out her breath like a horse.

She was walking quickly now, out in the open,

forgetting that she might have to slip into the shrubbery and hide. Then suddenly Johnny turned up a walkway, and she stopped. She moved silently into the neighboring yard, pausing in the shadows when the moon came from behind the clouds.

When she was safely behind a hedge, she stopped. Johnny was waiting at the foot of the steps. He shifted impatiently, glanced up at the house, wiped his hands on his shirt. When the front door opened, he moved back into the shadows, then he came forward as he saw Arthur step out.

Arthur. Retta's mouth drew into a sneer as she said the name to herself. At that moment she hated her brother and Arthur equally. The boys spoke to each other quietly, heads together. Arthur must be slipping out, too, she thought with the same sense of disgust.

Suddenly the boys started walking away. Arthur shifted a bag of equipment from one arm to the other. Johnny offered to carry it. Arthur shook his head.

Retta was so intent on not losing her brother that she plunged through the hedge, coming out on the other side with swimming motions. She barely felt the scratches on her arms and legs. She scrambled to her feet.

Ahead, Arthur was talking and Johnny nodding in agreement. They won't get away with this,

Retta promised herself. Now Arthur was explaining something in a low voice. Johnny lifted his hand and waved it in a wide arc. He was almost skipping with excitement. He laughed.

Every movement, every word, made Retta angrier, and the more excited Johnny became, the more Retta wanted to ruin that excitement. It was all she could do to keep from running forward, grabbing his arm, and shaking away his joy.

"I'll teach you not to slip out at night," she would say. "I won't have this kind of behavior!" She forgot that it was she herself who had taught him to slip out in the first place.

Johnny and Arthur did not glance back. Johnny was walking sideways now, facing Arthur so he wouldn't miss anything Arthur said or did. Retta was moving through the yards, keeping close to trees and shrubbery even though she felt Johnny would not notice her even if she walked openly in the street.

The street came to a dead end, and the boys cut through a vacant lot. Retta moved closer. Without the street lights it was harder to keep them in sight.

Retta stumbled over a child's lawn mower that had been left in the weeds. She fell forward. She remained face down for a moment, afraid they might have heard her.

When she raised her head, she saw they were moving up the hill, unaware of anything but themselves. "I could have broken my neck and they wouldn't notice," she muttered as she got to her feet. Her eyes were hard, her lips set.

Up the hill the boys were now in the clearing. They moved to the top of the hill and paused. Retta stooped and began to crawl toward them. There were few bushes and no trees, and she was determined not to be noticed until she was ready. Still stooping, she moved around the hill and came up behind them.

Arthur and Johnny were bent forward, backs to her, when she came over the crest of the hill. She eased herself onto her stomach and lay watching them.

Their backs hid what they were doing, but Retta did not dare move closer. They had some sort of plastic dry cleaning bag—she could see that—and Johnny was holding one end in the air.

"Is that right?" he asked.

"Yes."

Arthur was kneeling, striking matches, shielding them from the evening breeze with his hand. He was lighting something. Retta got to her knees. She had to see what he was doing.

In the opening of the plastic bag was a wire circle with narrow strips of wood across it. The strips of wood were covered with little candles. Arthur lit the candles quickly, lighting new matches from the burning candles. When all the candles were lit, the bag began to fill with hot air.

Retta stood. She was glad they were playing with fire because that was something no mother allowed.

The bag was filled now. The candles glowed eerily in the night. "It's getting ready to go," Arthur said. Johnny stepped back, hands clasped together with excitement.

Retta took one step forward as the bag rose into the air. Her shoulders were straight. The fact that what the boys were doing could be dangerous gave her extra strength. With her hands on her hips, she started across the clearing.

The bag was rising rapidly now, shooting up into the cool night air. Both boys' faces were turned skyward.

Retta moved toward them. She was not running. She had all the time in the world.

"Look how high it is!" Johnny cried. At that moment Retta reached him. She paused a moment, watching him. His hands were clasped beneath his chin, his face turned upward.

Abruptly Retta grabbed him by the upper arm and spun him around. "What do you think you're doing?" she snapped.

Johnny's mouth fell open. He drew back instinctively. Retta clutched his arm tighter.

"I said, what are you doing?"

Johnny had no answer. His mouth had gone dry. His knees were weak. He drew in a long, shuddering breath as if it were his last.

Retta pointed to the hot-air bag. It was descending now down the hill. It hovered over a tree and then rose as the candles reheated the air. Retta had a renewed flash of anger that the candles had not set the tree on fire. That would have really proved her point.

Arthur moved toward them then, and Retta turned back to her brother. She shook him as fiercely as an animal shakes its prey. Johnny did not struggle. He allowed himself to be shaken.

Suddenly Retta wanted to make his actions look as bad as possible. She leaned forward, including Arthur in her dark glance. "What are you trying to do?" she yelled. "Burn down the whole city?"

"I don't see what you're so upset about," Arthur was saying. The three of them were walking down the sidewalk with Retta in the lead. "We didn't do any harm."

"You almost caught a tree and a house on fire," Retta said. "You don't think that's harm?"

She had been determined at first not to speak to Arthur at all in order to show her contempt for him, but she had not been able to do that. She was condescending to answer his questions now, but over her shoulder, as if he were a servant.

"I don't get it," Arthur went on. "It's all right for your brothers to slip out at night with *you*, but—"

"*I* don't start fires," she said.

"I don't either. Did I start a fire?" When Retta

did not answer, he directed the question to Johnny. "Did we start a fire?"

He turned to look at Johnny, who was trailing behind them, but Johnny did not look up.

"You did not start a fire," Retta said in what she considered a mature voice, "because you were fortunate enough to have the candles burn out in the air."

Johnny was walking slower now. With each step he fell farther behind. His head sank forward in misery. The backs of his legs had a weak feeling that made walking difficult.

Retta's appearance at the very moment of his triumph had been as shocking and sudden as that of a wicked witch. Indeed, she had been so witch-like in her actions and voice that it had seemed a remake of that scene in *The Wizard of Oz* when the Wicked Witch of the West appears in a puff of red smoke.

He had a helpless feeling. It was as if he were a puppet, and his sister would always be there, pulling the strings, spying on him, waiting for just the right moment to leap forward and spoil his life.

Ahead, Arthur was saying, "I don't see why you have to treat your brothers like prisoners!"

"*You* wouldn't," Retta said over her shoulder. Then, realizing she had made a mistake, she added quickly, "Anyway, I do *not* treat them like prisoners."

"Yes, you do."

"I do not!"

She swirled suddenly to face him. Caught off-guard, Arthur almost bumped into her.

"I happen to be in charge of my brothers," Retta said. Her hands were on her hips now. She felt strong enough, mature enough, to be put on a Mother's Day card. "I cook for them and I wash their clothes and I see that they go to bed and I even do their homework for them, and they are not prisoners!"

"And do you think for them too?"

Retta turned abruptly. She began walking rapidly down the sidewalk.

"Look, I didn't mean to upset you," Arthur said.

"You couldn't upset me."

"It's just that we really weren't doing anything wrong."

"Huh!"

"Anyway, what we were doing wasn't any worse than swimming in somebody's pool without permission."

"That's *your* opinion."

Johnny was lagging even farther behind. As soon as he had heard Arthur use the word "prisoner," he had realized that was what he was. Tears stung his eyes, and he was grateful for the dark and for the distance between him and Arthur.

He realized that his friendship with Arthur was ruined—it had been too good to be true anyway—but he did not want Arthur to see him cry. To see him treated like a baby was bad enough. He be-

gan to drag his feet on the sidewalk, pausing every now and then to stand, arms hanging, and look at the ground.

"Isn't that your house?" Retta asked Arthur over her shoulder.

"Yes."

"Well, shouldn't you go in? We would like to walk home by ourselves, if you don't mind."

"I do mind. I'm not one of your brothers, you know. You can't boss me around."

Arthur stopped and waited for Johnny to join him. Johnny, head down, said, "Go on in. You don't have to worry about me."

"Well, I just don't feel right about what happened," Arthur said, lowering his voice.

"Me either."

"If only your sister would listen to reason."

"She won't."

"It's not like we did anything wrong."

"I know, but that's the way she is."

"Stop talking about me," Retta snapped. She was standing apart from them, waiting. She kept her back to them as if they were too unimportant to notice.

"Well, that *is* the way you are," Johnny said. Arthur's presence at his side made him feel stronger. He glanced up at Arthur for the first time since his sister's arrival. "Everything always has to be her way. She always has to be the boss."

"I got that."

"Nothing we want matters."

Arthur glanced at Retta's unyielding back. He said, "Well, maybe she really cares about you guys, only she just doesn't know how to—"

Retta spun around, eyes blazing. With the moonlight shining on her, she looked taller than either of the boys. She looked at Arthur with such loathing that he moved back a step.

"Don't you dare say anything nice about me!" she yelled.

Retta knew something was wrong as soon as she rounded the corner of her block. The porch light was on, and a strange car was parked in front of their house.

"Something's happened," she said. She began to run up the hill toward the house.

Behind her Arthur and Johnny sensed something too. They moved faster, closing the distance between them. The three of them reached the porch steps at the same time, but Retta beat them through the front door. It was she who saw the colonel first.

She stopped so abruptly that Johnny bumped into her and shoved her to the center of the room. Then Johnny saw the colonel, too, and drew back,

leaving Retta standing alone. He had only had a
brief look at the colonel before—and the colonel
had been wearing shorty pajamas at the time—but
he knew this was the colonel. He let out his breath
in a long, uneasy sigh.

The colonel sat with his hands on his legs in a
pose that looked military. Beside him, crumpled
into a ball, lay Roy. He had cried himself to sleep
and now lay still, wrapped in one of the colonel's
flannel shirts, drawing an occasional shuddering
breath.

Roy had been, from that first illegal swim,
afraid of the colonel. It was the kind of unreason-
able fear usually saved for ghosts and wolves and
two-headed giants. And in his one dramatic meet-
ing with the colonel tonight, the colonel had
seemed to live up to expectations.

The colonel had been so big, so stern, so all-
powerful as he stood above Roy that Roy had
quivered with fear. His hands, reaching for him,
had looked as big as hams, and his eyes seemed to
glow red.

At the same time Roy himself seemed to be
shrinking. It was as dramatic a sensation as something out of science fiction. He could actually feel
himself getting smaller. He half expected to disap-
pear.

This miracle had not happened, however, and
he found himself forced into the colonel's house,
forced into dry clothes (that was how he thought
of it), forced to tell his name and address. Then—

this was worse than being arrested—he was driven home.

As the car had pulled up to the curb in front of his house, Roy had had a brief hope that the colonel would let him go with a stern warning. He tried to get out of the car with a strangled "Thank you for the ride," but politeness did not work.

The colonel unbuckled his seat belt. He got out of the car. On the way up the walk the colonel said the most terrible words Roy had ever heard in his life: "I want to talk to your father."

Now Retta looked from the colonel to Roy. When her eyes met the colonel's a second time, she straightened her shoulders. "What happened?"

"Are you his sister?"

"Yes. I take care of him."

"You weren't taking very good care of him tonight. He almost drowned."

"What?"

"He came swimming alone. He jumped into the deep end of the pool and he can't swim. If I hadn't been there, he would have drowned."

"Oh, no."

Retta stood in the center of the room. She felt as if the middle part of the room had suddenly shifted, leaving her off-balance. She reached out for something to steady her, but she felt only air.

"I called your father," the colonel said. "He should be here any minute."

Retta stepped back. She put up one hand as if to stop whatever the colonel was going to say next.

The colonel turned to Johnny. "Who's in charge of you kids?"

"*She* is," Johnny said.

Retta closed her eyes. When she opened them, she saw Roy lying on the sofa. Suddenly she realized how young, how vulnerable, he was. She looked at Johnny, who was standing shoulder to shoulder with Arthur. She felt as bewildered as a child whose dolls have come to life and are demanding real care and attention.

"I don't know how all this happened," Retta said, more to herself than to the colonel.

"Well," the colonel said, "it happened because—" He broke off.

There were footsteps on the porch, and Shorty Anderson appeared in the doorway in his hot-pink cowboy suit with the rhinestone lapels. Tears sprang to Retta's eyes, turning Shorty into a glittering pink circle. As she watched, her father seemed to swirl away like a Frisbee, moving far out of reach in an eddy of glittering lights.

She blinked and he was, once again, there in the doorway. Just as Roy had looked younger than she remembered, her father now seemed older. The pink velour suit looked a little tight, worn at the seams. Tears came to her eyes again, and this time they spilled onto her cheeks.

The colonel moved to the doorway. "Mr. Anderson?" he asked. The colonel was so tall he could have been Shorty Anderson's father. Shorty Anderson took three steps forward in his high-heeled boots.

Johnny and Arthur pulled back the way bystanders in cowboy movies retreat to safety. Arthur groped for the doorknob behind him.

The colonel put out his hand. "I'm Colonel Roberts. The kids have been swimming in my pool at night."

Shorty Anderson took the colonel's hand. "At night?" he asked. He looked blankly from the colonel to his children. "Aren't they in bed at night?"

The colonel shook his head. "They've been coming over and swimming in our pool after we go to bed. It's not that we mind them swimming there, but it's dangerous and we're responsible. Tonight the little boy almost drowned."

"You kids have been doing this?" Shorty Anderson asked Retta.

She nodded, unable to speak.

"Johnny?"

"Yes."

Shorty Anderson looked at his youngest son on the sofa. Roy stirred. He opened his eyes and saw that he was no longer alone with the colonel. Indeed, the room seemed to be filled with people.

Blinking with sleep, Roy struggled to sit up. He remembered why he and the colonel were here—to have a talk with his father. The horror of the eve-

ning washed over him again. He stood up on the
sofa, tottering on the uneven cushions. He
clutched the colonel's wrinkled shirt tightly, as if
to give himself extra support.

Then, in a voice trembling with self-pity, he an-
nounced, "It was her fault." He pointed at Retta.
He had spoken without thinking, but he saw suddenly it was the truth. Unwittingly he had hit on
the real reason they were all standing here. He
summed it up in three words. "She left me!"

Retta stepped back. Everyone was looking at
her. She made a gesture with her hand and
knocked over Shorty Anderson's lamp. In the silence that followed the shattering of glass, Shorty
Anderson sighed. He looked around him like a
man who has just discovered the sun rising in the
west. He glanced up at the colonel, down at his
broken lamp.

For a moment he seemed to get even shorter.
Then he straightened. "Maybe we better sit down
and talk," he said in a tired voice.

"Now, honey, it's not all that bad," Brendelle said. She had arrived as the colonel was leaving, and she now sat in the kitchen with Retta.

"Yes, it is," Retta said. She began to pull at one of the worn spots Roy had made in the tablecloth.

"No, it's not. Now, listen. Nobody got drowned. Nobody got hurt. Nobody's been arrested." Brendelle began to tick off their blessings as if they were the lyrics to a song. "And best of all, maybe now that sorry father of yours will take better care of you. You hear me, Shorty?"

"What?" he called from the living room.

"I was just saying that, well, now maybe these kids' sorry father will take better care of them. Did you hear me?"

Silence.

"What these kids need is a mother. You hear me, Shorty?"

Silence.

"You ought to find yourself a nice girl and get married," Brendelle suggested.

Silence.

"Though I don't guess they'd be a whole lot of nice girls who'd want you. As a matter of fact," she winked at Retta, "I can't think of but one!" She waited; when there was no answer, she reached out and put her hand over Retta's. Retta looked up and Brendelle said, "It *is* going to be all right."

"I just don't know what I did wrong."

"You didn't do anything wrong." She shook her head. "Okay, you went swimming where you weren't supposed to. But, honey, look, everybody does that. Why, when we were graduating from high school we had this dance and afterwards we all climbed over the fence around the municipal pool and went swimming in our evening clothes."

"Did you?"

"My mom almost killed me because I had on a new pink formal that cost thirty-five dollars and it was ruined. One boy had on a rented tuxedo and he wouldn't go in so we threw him in. And that tuxedo—they don't use good dye on them or something—that tuxedo turned the swimming pool water *purple*. Would you believe it? And when he got out, everywhere he stood he made a purple puddle and nobody would let him ride home in their car."

Retta was picking at the tablecloth again. She said, "I just don't see how mothers do it."

"What?"

"Oh, I don't know. Take care of kids and have them turn out right. I mean, I can see how you can be a good mother if you're there all the time saying, 'Stop that,' and, 'Don't do this.' But when they get away from you, well, I just don't see how mothers do it."

"I don't know either, hon. When it comes to mothering I'm as green as grass. But I do know one thing—you can't hold too tight. As soon as you start holding on so tight that somebody knows they're being held—well, then you're in trouble."

Retta sighed. "You know something? I've been hating my brothers all week."

"You didn't really hate them, hon."

"Yes, I did."

"Let me tell you something. My sister Rhonda and I, well, we are really close now. We talk on the phone three times a week and she lives in Ohio. Anyway, last year we were going through some old stuff at Mom's and I found a diary of mine. The whole diary was how much I hated Rhonda. Rhonda got to do everything. Rhonda had the good clothes. Rhonda this. Rhonda that. 'I hate Rhonda' was on every page. Honey, I wrote the word 'hate' so hard that fifteen years later the page was still dented." She took Retta's hands across the table. "You'll get over it."

"I already am over it, I guess." Retta smiled for the first time that day. "Everything I say, you say the same thing happened to you."

"That's because everything has happened to me. Everything but one thing." She raised her voice, grinning at Retta. "Nobody ever asked me to marry them. That's the only thing that hasn't happened to me. You hear that, Shorty?"

"I heard."

"You think anybody ever will, Shorty?"

"Maybe. There's a lot of fools in this world."

"It don't take but one."

Retta looked at Brendelle. For the first time she understood that Brendelle and her father might really get married.

"What's wrong?" Brendelle asked. "I turn away and you look all right and I turn back and you've got a funny look on your face."

"It was just something I thought of."

"Something bad?"

"No."

"Well, that's good because we have had enough bad thoughts around here for one night." She turned back to the door. "Shorty, come on in here with us. I'll fix something to eat."

There was no answer.

"*Shorty?*"

Shorty Anderson was sitting in the living room. The evening had been so upsetting that he had not taken off his pink velour suit. The telephone call from the colonel, summoning him home from the Downtown Hoedown, had frightened him. And the sight of his children—who looked smaller, somehow, paler than he remembered—had not made him feel any better.

It seemed to him that every time his life started getting good, something bad happened.

His song, "You're Fifty Pounds Too Much Woman for Me," was on the charts, and now, just when he wanted to devote his full time to making it a hit, the burdens of fatherhood fell upon him. It made him feel so low he didn't even want to write a song about it.

"Shorty, did you hear me calling you?"

"I heard." He got up slowly, walked into the kitchen, and opened the refrigerator door.

Brendelle watched him. "I hope you're not planning to eat while you've got on that suit," she said. "You know how you spill stuff. One spot of mayo and that pink velour is ruined."

Se stood tiredly at the refrigerator.

"Now you go take off that suit and I'll fix you a sandwich. What kind you want?"

"Fried egg." Obediently he started for his room.

"Coming up. Retta, you want one too?"

"No, thanks."

"Then you go on to bed. Somebody's got to start giving orders around here."

Retta nodded. She got to her feet. "Good night, Brendelle."

"Good night, hon." She hugged Retta to her. "And you sleep late in the morning. That's another order. I'll fix a bunch of fried egg sandwiches and put them in the fridge. You can have them for breakfast."

"Do they keep?" Retta asked. Suddenly she began to feel her own fatigue.

"Hon, they get better. The grease goes right through the bread and when you toast them—well, you just wait till in the morning and see."

"All right."

Retta left the kitchen and paused in the hallway. Her father was standing in his room, in front of the mirror, having one last look at himself in his pink suit before he took it off. He turned sideways. The sight of himself in velour, a star's material, made him feel a little better. His fatigue began to ease.

Watching himself, he sang, "When you get eatin' off of your mind, I'll get cheatin' off of mine. I don't want no extry woman in my aaaaaarms."

He caught sight of Retta watching him and said, "Did I tell you 'Fifty Pounds Too Much Woman' is number eighty-nine on the charts?"

She nodded. "I hope it goes all the way for you."

"Oh, hon, me too." He came out into the hall. His energy was returning. Grabbing Retta, he square-danced her into the living room. He steered her through the dining room, into the kitchen, around the table, back into the hall.

Brendelle called, "Shorty, you are supposed to be changing and Retta is supposed to be going to bed."

"First things first," Shorty Anderson called back. "I'm dancing with my daughter."

He swung Retta around in the hall, turning her until she was dizzy. Then, still humming to himself, he released her, danced alone into his bedroom, and began taking off his pink velour suit.

Standing in the hallway, still slightly dizzy, Retta had a funny feeling. Everything had changed and yet nothing had changed. It was like those stories where a person is whisked away to a different time zone, lives a whole different life, and then returns to find that no time has elapsed at all, that everyone is still in exactly the same place.

She glanced into her brothers' room. They were asleep. She walked softly into the room. Roy stirred and lifted his head.

"Is that you, Retta?"

"Yes."

"What are you doing?"

"Nothing. Just standing here."

"You can get in bed with me if you want to." This was Roy's peace offering. He could not imag-

ine anything lonelier than having to get in a bed
by yourself.

"All right. For a minute."

Roy wiggled to the edge of the bed, and Retta
crawled over the foot and slid between Roy and
Johnny. She turned onto her back. The mattress
springs rattled comfortingly.

"What will we do tomorrow, Retta?" Roy asked
sleepily, more out of habit than because he
wanted to know.

"Oh, I don't know." She swallowed. "I imagine
Johnny will go play with Arthur and you'll go play
with somebody. I don't know exactly." She
paused. "Is there anything really *special* that
you'd like to do tomorrow?"

There was something final about the way Retta
asked the question. It was as if what they would
do tomorrow, this special thing, would mark the
end of something.

He looked at Retta. She was staring up at the
ceiling. In the light from the hall, her face had a
strange, still expression. For a moment she looked
so much like his mother that he held his breath.
He noticed for the first time that Retta had the
same nose, the same full bottom lip, the same stat-
uelike eyes as his mother. And the hall light almost seemed to be a spotlight, highlighting her
features.

The last time Roy could remember actually
seeing his mother, she had been on the stage, lit
up so that everyone in the audience could see her

while he, in the wings, looked at her profile. He blinked, and abruptly he was back in his bed, acutely aware that Retta was just his sister.

"*Is* there something you'd like to do?" Retta asked.

"The Bowlwater plant," he said almost without thinking.

She looked at him and he shifted his head. Now it was he who was staring at the ceiling. "Retta?"

"What?"

"The Bowlwater plant—is it a great big plant with leaves and giant flowers and stuff?"

"No."

He took a deep breath. The wind wasn't blowing in the right direction, but he thought he smelled the Bowlwater plant for the last time. He exhaled.

"It's a factory, isn't it?" he asked.

"Yes."

"And there aren't any giant plants with giant leaves, are there?"

"Maybe in the jungle, Roy. I don't know."

"Yes, in the jungle, or maybe on other planets. There could be giant plants on other planets."

"That's right."

"But not around here."

"No."

A satisifed feeling came over Roy as he lay there. It was as if, by swallowing a hard truth about life as willingly—this was the way he saw it—as Popeye swallows spinach, he had become stronger. "There are no giant plants around here," he said again, feeling better every time he confirmed the unhappy fact.

Retta rose up on one elbow to look at him, remembering his hopes for the Bowlwater plant as a kind of recreational facility, a natural Disney World where everything was real instead of plastic. He seemed almost pleased as he lay there with the covers pulled up to his chin. Maybe each of us, she thought, had been off into that strange time zone that changes a person while keeping the rest of the world the same.

"Well, I better go to bed," she said. "It's three o'clock in the morning." She hugged Roy. "Good night."

She turned over and hugged Johnny. Johnny stirred. He was drawn out of a dream in which he and Arthur, grown men, were sending rockets off to planets as yet unnamed. He squirmed with irritation and said, "Let go of me."

"I have," Retta said.

"Retta, you can hug me all you want to. I don't care how many times you hug me," Roy said.

"Thanks."

She climbed off the foot of the bed and started for her room. In the hallway she bumped into her father, shorter than she now, without his cowboy boots. "Doesn't anybody ever go to bed around here?" he asked.

"I'm going."

She went into her room and got under the covers without bothering to take off her clothes. She sighed. She was as tired as if she'd been working in the fields.

She could hear Brendelle talking in the kitchen. "Here's your sandwich."

Shorty Anderson said, "You know, that's not a bad line for a song."

"What? 'Here's your sandwich'?"

"No, what you said earlier when you were hollering at me in the living room. I said, 'There's a lot of fools in this world,' and you said, 'It don't take but one.'"

Brendelle said, "Now, look. Aren't you glad you changed? You already got egg yolk on your shirt. If that had been velour, well . . ."

Shorty said, "Hand me a napkin." There was the sound of rustling as he tucked it into his shirt collar. "Now, listen to this, Brendelle."

"I'm listening."

He began to sing. "It don't take but one fool and you got a fool in me. It don't—"

"Shorty Anderson, didn't anybody ever teach you to hold your hand under a fried egg sandwich while you're eating?"

"I'm sorry, hon, hand me another napkin."

"Here's two."

There was more rustling. Then Shorty said, "Wait a minute. Would this be better? Something like 'You Got Sixteen Kinds of Fools in Me.'"

"That's not bad."

He began to sing again. "You got a fool who loves you and a fool who'll let you go." A pause. "You got a fool who needs you but who don't want it to show. You got a fool who'll be around through good times and through bad, and a fool who'll—"

He broke off. "I'm going to get my guitar."

"I'll get it, hon," Brendelle said.

And in the comfortable silence that followed, Retta fell asleep.